"What do you think of me?"

Lucas's question took Shelley by surprise. She shifted in her chair. The night touched him, pulling him into the shadows, but she could see the look on his face. He was serious.

"You? You're a protector of people, a man who doesn't like to give pain. I think you're honorable and loyal, and you think that anyone who messes with your version of the law should be shot at dawn."

That brought a rough burst of laughter. He tossed back the last of his drink then put the glass on the table between them.

"Shot at dawn?" he murmured in a low voice. "I hardly think that's the fate I'd prescribe for you."

The mood was shifting so quickly that Shelley could barely breathe, but she couldn't keep from uttering the question. "What would you prescribe for me?"

He was very still, his eyes never leaving her face. "I'm your bodyguard, Shelley. I'm here to guard your body. There's only one place I can be sure it's safe...."

ABOUT THE AUTHOR

Mary Anne Wilson lives in Southern California with her husband, three children, two exceptional grandchildren and an odd assortment of dysfunctional pets. She has been a Rita Award finalist for outstanding romantic suspense, makes regular appearances on the Waldenbooks bestseller list and has been a Reviewer's Choice nominee for *Romantic Times* magazine. She believes real love is a rare and precious gift— the greatest mystery in life.

Books by Mary Anne Wilson

HARLEQUIN AMERICAN ROMANCE

MARY ANNE WILSON

HER BODYGUARD

Harlequin Books

TORONTO • NEW YORK • LONDON
AMSTERDAM • PARIS • SYDNEY • HAMBURG
STOCKHOLM • ATHENS • TOKYO • MILAN
MADRID • WARSAW • BUDAPEST • AUCKLAND

For Tom with love,
for being the "Keeper of the Flame"
for more years than either of us
dreamed

ISBN 0-373-16543-9

HER BODYGUARD

Copyright © 1994 by Mary Anne Wilson

Prologue

The members of the San Francisco Police Department stood in full dress uniform on a grassy knoll that overlooked the bay in the old cemetery. Lucas Jordon, one of the ranks, stood behind them, his dark eyes narrowed at the grayness of the day and his body numb to the cold mist falling from a leaden sky.

He stood amid the old granite headstones by the fresh grave, near the back of the mourners, the canvas sling and heavy bandages on his left arm and shoulder covered partially by a dark overcoat. He'd thought about wearing his dress blues but knew there was no way he could have managed to put them on. Having one good hand stopped him from doing a lot more things than working.

Lucas didn't hate easily. He'd learned a long time ago that hate was a useless emotion. But at that moment as the first rifle report rang through the gray mists, he knew he could hate the person responsible for letting Monroe back on the streets, a person who made a career at the public defender's office using the law to get the guilty freed.

Captain Richard Bentley, a slightly built man, spoke about Larry Hall, a man Bentley had entered the academy with eighteen years ago. A good cop who shouldn't have died in a drug raid at a flophouse near the docks at the hands of a career criminal.

But all Lucas could think was, *It shouldn't have happened.*

He knew the ironies of being a cop after fifteen years of service. He was a walking irony. Just two weeks before Larry Hall had died, Lucas had been the one to catch a bullet. It had shattered bones, torn up his shoulder and severed nerves. If it had been four inches to the right, it would have caught his lungs and heart and he would have been the one dead. And the worst irony of all was the fact that the man who shot him shouldn't have been on the streets. Not any more than Freddy Monroe should have been on the streets to kill Larry Hall.

Despite the fact he couldn't even form a fist with his left hand, pain burned through him with a life of its own. It radiated from his left arm into his neck and back, and as he clenched his jaw he could feel a cold sweat breaking out on his forehead. The painkillers were wearing off.

He slowly looked around the gathering of mourners as the honor guard raised their rifles into the air. He skimmed over faces of grief but stopped when he spotted a woman across from him standing back from the cluster of mourners partially under the outspread boughs of an old sycamore tree.

She was pale, with silvery blond hair skimmed back from a high-cheekboned face. A dark coat highlighted her wan complexion. But she was lovely in a delicate way. He looked away quickly, shaken by the idea that if he lost his arm, he wouldn't be able to really hold a woman again.

He swallowed hard. And the hatred he'd felt just moments ago came back full force. He closed his eyes, let the cool mists touch his face, and he heard the gunshots of the salute echo in the darkness.

WITH EACH SUCCESSIVE shot fired by the honor guard, Shelley Kingston flinched. She hated guns. She hated violence. And she didn't know why she'd come here today, except she knew she had to. She stood off from the others, not part of the crowd of mourners with their scattering of umbrellas being raised against the mists. She knew that she really had no place here.

She stayed under the shelter of the spreading branches of the old tree and tugged her dark coat more tightly around her. When she'd heard about the shoot-out, that a cop had been killed during a drug arrest, she'd felt terrible. And when she'd heard the name of the dead gunman who'd shot down the cop, she'd felt sick.

Intellectually, she knew she wasn't to blame. As part of the staff at the public defender's office, she'd done her job and used the law given to her. But she also knew that no one here would accept or believe that.

As the shots rang in the cold air, she started to turn away and head to her car. But she paused when she caught sight of a man across the way, on the fringes of the mourners. A dark man with a dark overcoat draped over his shoulders. He stood rigidly, his eyes closed, his jaw clenched.

She looked away quickly, turning to start for the car. She could almost feel pain radiating from the man, and she couldn't look at it. As she hurried across the spongy grass, she knew she wouldn't come to another funeral like this. She had no place here.

ONE OF THE MOURNERS stood in the middle of the gathering, sharing an umbrella, but isolated nonetheless. Shelley Kingston wasn't aware, but eyes watched her as she left. The last volley from the rifles echoed in the cold air.

Then the mourner turned and stared at the casket under the feeble protection of a white canopy that had been hurriedly set up when the rains started. Everything blurred, the red, white and blue of the flag running together. Everything seemed out of focus and wrong, except the hate.

Hate gave meaning to a meaningless situation. But hating Freddy Monroe was useless. His life wasn't enough payment for Larry being gone. Knowing Monroe had died from a shot by Larry's gun seconds after he'd shot Larry wasn't enough. A street-punk junkie was too little payment for the cop and man Larry had been.

But suddenly payment had shown up at the funeral. Shelley Kingston. She was the woman responsible for all of this. And in that second the mourner knew that Shelley Kingston was going to be payment in full for Larry's life . . . one way or another.

Chapter One

December 20

When Shelley finally got home, it was late, almost seven o'clock, and a chilly breeze was whipping in off the distant San Francisco Bay. She and her daughter hurried up the front porch steps of the old bungalow they rented south of the city, and just as she pushed the key in the brass lock of the front door, she heard the phone start to ring.

She didn't want to talk to Ryan Sullivan, her superior at the office. She'd talked to him enough today, and she didn't want to keep arguing with him about the right plea for a street kid who accidentally got involved in a holdup. As she opened the door, Emily rushed past her into the shadowy house and called over her shoulder, "I'll get it."

"I'm busy," Shelley called after her. "Take a message and tell them I'll call them back later."

Shelley stepped into the house and swung the door shut as Emily turned on the kitchen light. The yellow glow spilled into the living room, exposing hardwood floors, scattered braided rugs and well-used wicker furniture.

As she heard Emily say, "Hello, Kingston residence," she flipped on a table lamp by the white wicker couch and dropped her briefcase and purse on one of the chairs grouped around the stone fireplace.

"She's busy, may I take a message?" Emily was saying politely.

Shelley stepped out of the black pumps she was wearing with a simple navy suit and started across the room that ran the width of the house. She stepped through the arch onto the cold linoleum floor in the old-fashioned kitchen while she debated with herself about ordering pizza or trying to find something in the refrigerator to fix for dinner.

Tugging the clip out of her blond hair as she crossed to the sinks that sat under a bank of windows at the back of the room, she freed the shoulder-length mane from the low knot she always confined it to at work. As she combed her fingers through her hair, she glanced at Emily standing on a low wooden stool by the wall phone near the laundry room door.

In a green jumper and white blouse, with wheat-blond hair caught in two braids off her finely featured face, she looked incredibly tiny for seven years old. Usually a nonstop talker, she was listening intently to whatever was being said on the other end of the phone.

A frown tugged a fine line between lavender blue eyes that echoed her mother's shade. "No, he doesn't," she finally said as she started twisting one of her braids around and around her finger.

"Of course, I can remember," she said as she rolled her eyes upward and exhaled. "My mother lets me take messages."

Shelley knew it was stupid to be trying to sidestep Ryan. She'd have to deal with the problems sooner or later, and she was just about ready to brace herself and cross to take the phone when Emily said, "Okay. Merry Christmas, too," and put the phone in the cradle.

She jumped off the stool, her scuffed oxfords landing squarely on the floor, and headed toward the refrigerator. "Emily, who was that?" Shelley asked.

"I don't know." Emily opened the refrigerator door and reached inside, then turned with a can of soda in her hand. "They didn't say what their name was. Just that they wanted to talk to you. But I told them you were busy and I had to take a message."

Shelley automatically reached to take the can of soda. "Not before dinner," she said absentmindedly. "Wasn't it Mr. Sullivan from my office?"

"No." Emily looked at the soda in Shelley's hand. "I'm thirsty," she said with a slight whine that came when she was tired. It had been a long day for her, with school and the after-school program she attended until Shelley could come and get her after work.

That too-familiar feeling of shortchanging her daughter came to taunt her, but Shelley killed it with the realistic answer that she had to work hard right now. Once she'd completed two years with the public defender's office she could get into a good law firm, then Emily would have everything she needed. There would be good hours, money to do what they wanted to do, and they wouldn't have to depend on child support that seldom came on time... if it came at all.

In an attempt to appease both of them, she said, "Let's get pizza tonight," as she put the pop can on the counter.

Emily immediately brightened. "Yeah, pizza, with lots of sausage and no mushrooms."

Shelley crouched down in front of her daughter, getting to her eye level. "That sounds good, but before I call for pizza, tell me about the phone call. Who was it?"

"I don't know."

"Was it a man or a woman?"

"I couldn't tell."

"All right. What did they tell you?" she asked, her patience wearing thin.

"They wanted to know if my father was here."

That took her aback. "What?"

"They just asked me if he was here, and I told them no."

Shelley had been careful to tell Emily to never give out information over the phone to strangers. But she'd never thought about her telling anyone about the lack of a father in the home. "What else did they say?"

"That they had a message for you and could I remember it?"

"Do you remember it?"

"Of course, I do." She frowned intently as she concentrated. "I'm supposed to tell you that they know that you get proper..." She shook her head sharply, making her braids dance around her shoulders. "No, popertaters off."

"Perpetrators?"

"Yeah, that's it. You get those off, but it's a bad thing, and you won't get away with it anymore, 'cause they won't let you and you gotta pay."

Shelley felt as if she'd been struck in the stomach, but she tried to keep her voice calm. "Anything else?"

"No. Is something wrong? Did I get it mixed up?"

She wished to God the child had it all wrong. "No, I think you got it right."

"What does it mean?"

She considered lying, but couldn't. She was as truthful with Emily as she could possibly be. She'd learned a long time ago that lies eventually hurt worse than the truth. They never solved anything, not any more than pretending did. "I've been having some problems at the office."

"It's Mr. Sullivan, isn't it? He doesn't like you."

"No, it's not Mr. Sullivan. We like each other just fine. We just have arguments from time to time. But he's pretty decent. This is different."

"What is it?"

She pressed her hands on her thighs. "You know the kind of people I deal with at the office?"

"Sure."

"There are some good ones, but from time to time I have to deal with people who aren't very nice. In the past couple of weeks I've been getting letters and phone calls from someone. They don't like me, and they think I'm doing the wrong thing."

Emily shifted from foot to foot, obviously bored with the explanation before Shelley could get it all out. "Then put them in jail," she said with infinite logic.

"That's just it. I don't know who they are. They never sign their names or tell anyone who's calling. I think the person who just called and talked to you is the one doing it at work."

Emily's eyes widened. "Really? They didn't sound mad on the phone or mean or anything. They even said 'Merry Christmas.'"

"You know that I always try to be honest with you."

"Sure, but Stanley Weed at school says that I'm stupid because I was honest with him and told him there isn't any Santa Claus. He wants to fight me, and I told him that I'd fight him, but it had to be fair, and that he had to—"

"Emily, please, we'll talk about Stanley Weed and Santa Claus later. Right now, I'm worried about that call. Whoever made it, they have our private number. So from now on, don't answer the phone. Okay?"

"But I like to do it," she said, the whine coming back into her voice. "You said I did it good, real good, too."

"And you do. But for the next few days, I need to do it myself, in case that person calls back. Do you understand?"

She nodded. "I guess so."

"Good, now I'm going to call Mr. Sullivan and tell him about the call you answered, then I'll call and order pizza."

"What's Mr. Sullivan going to do?"

"I don't know."

"He should call the police and have them lock up the bad person so I can answer the phone again."

"That's a good idea, if life was only that simple," Shelley murmured as she brushed the wispy strands of pale hair at Emily's cheek that had worked free of the braids. "For now, I'll call Mr. Sullivan."

"Then the pizza?"

"Then the pizza," she said as she stood and crossed to the phone. But before she could touch the receiver, the phone rang. She stared at it as she felt Emily come to press against her right side.

"Are you going to answer it, Mommy?"

"Of course," she said and picked up the receiver. "Hello?"

"Hey, I thought you'd be ducking me," Ryan boomed over the line.

She didn't realize how nervous she'd been about answering it until she heard Ryan's voice. "Thank goodness it's you," she said, then put her hand over the receiver and whispered, "It's Mr. Sullivan," to Emily.

"Hey," Ryan was saying, "I like feeling welcome as much as the next guy, but you sound a bit desperate."

She took her hand off the receiver. "I guess I am." She quickly told him what happened, then said, "I was just about to call you to see what you thought about it."

"You know what they say about obscene phone callers and letter writers? They get off on that, and they seldom go any further. But I don't think we can take that chance now that they have your home phone number."

"I hate to pull in the police. Public defenders aren't their favorite people, and maybe I'm overreacting just a bit."

"Maybe. Maybe not. But we're citizens, just like anyone else, and the police are sworn to protect and serve. That includes PDs, no matter what they think about us. Why don't I call Dick Bentley and run it past him?"

"I guess it wouldn't hurt to talk to him about it and see what he thinks."

"I'll do that first thing in the morning. Oh, by the way, the reason I was calling was to tell you that I've decided to do what you want with the Charlie Moran case. We'll work out a deal you're happy with, then take it to the DA. With any luck we'll have his decision before Christmas."

She'd been pushing Ryan to go for a deal for the past week for the kid, and it should have given her pleasure. But nothing felt right just now. "That's great," she murmured. "I'd go for anything if he was eligible for probation."

"I don't know about that, but I'll find out and we'll discuss it in the morning."

"Thanks, Ryan," Shelley said, then slipped the receiver on the cradle. Maybe she was overreacting because of Emily being drawn into it. Maybe Ryan was right. Voyeurs seldom made direct contact. They vented their anger in letters and phone calls, not in person.

"Can we order pizza now?" Emily asked. "I'm so hungry."

Shelley looked at her daughter who was almost bouncing up and down with impatience. "Sure we can," she said, and jumped when the phone rang again. This time she reached for it without hesitating, thinking it was Ryan calling back with some information. But the second after she said, "Hey, Ryan, what did you forget?" she knew how wrong she was.

"This isn't Ryan, but you're Shelley Kingston, hotshot public defender, aren't you?" a raspy voice hissed in her ear. "You can't hide behind your kid. You're going to pay. I'll stop you *dead*."

Shelley slammed the receiver on the cradle with the crack of plastic on metal, then backed away. When the phone rang again almost immediately, she didn't move. Emily slipped her small hand into Shelley's and breathed, "It's that bad person, isn't it?"

"Yes," Shelley said and knew that she didn't really have a choice. She had to go to the police for help.

LUCAS FELT LIKE HELL, and it was one of his good days. His shoulder ached, his hand was stiff and not particularly responsive. But he knew he was lucky to even have a hand that would move, no matter how faulty that movement was.

He stood alone in his captain's office, and as he looked out the window at the San Francisco morning, he methodically squeezed and released a red exercise ball in his bad left hand. He saw wisps of fog that still clung to the downtown area, then beyond to the bay in the distance. Garlands and lights for Christmas were everywhere, and the morning traffic was backed up almost into Oakland.

He'd been off over two months, away from all of this, and he felt about ready to explode. Until he'd been shot, he hadn't thought too much about his life. He'd just lived it for thirty-five years. But two months of inactivity, being stuck in the apartment near the Presidio and staring at television without seeing what was on it, had pushed him near the edge.

He saw his reflection in the glass, a large, dark-haired, rough featured man who looked grim. And he felt grim. He'd thought too much about too many things, but one thing he knew—he wanted to work. He wanted to be busy and do something other than flip past soap operas in the afternoon and past game shows while he ate his dinner. And the long nights alone in bed . . .

"Hey, Lucas," someone said from behind him as a door clicked open and he turned to see Bentley stride into the room. "You beat me here," the thin, balding man said as he crossed to his desk and tossed a pile of papers onto the clutter already spread out there.

Dick hardly seemed the stereotypical cop, from his size to the clothes he favored, beiges and browns that washed him out and matched the color of what little hair he had left. He was a hard man to like, intense and demanding, but if he were liked or not, he was respected. Lucas always figured that was about all a man could ask for in this line of work.

"It's good to see you," Lucas said.

"I haven't seen you since . . ." His voice trailed off as he shrugged. "It's been a while."

"Yeah, it has," Lucas murmured, not about to say the word *funeral* out loud right now.

Dick dropped in his chair and swiveled to face Lucas by the windows, and he glanced at the hand squeezing the red ball. "How's it going?"

"Better. At least I still have an arm. And the doctor thinks I'll probably regain full use . . . in time."

"Good. Good." He started snapping a rubber band he was wearing on his wrist and grimaced. "This is supposed to stop me from wanting to smoke."

"Is it working?"

He shrugged and spun his chair around to face the desk. "It's bruising my wrist," he muttered, then reached for the papers he'd tossed on the desk when he came in.

Lucas went around the desk and dropped into one of the hard wooden chairs that faced the desk. "So, what's going on?"

The man sorted through the papers while he spoke. "A special assignment, something to ease you back into the work mode without giving you too much, too soon."

"I'll take it."

"Don't you want to know what it is?"

"I just want to work," he said honestly.

Dick tugged a sheet of paper clear of the others. "Ah, here we go." He pushed it across the desk to Lucas. "Take a look at this."

Lucas reached for the paper with his good hand, and as he turned it right side up he saw it was filled with an almost unreadable scrawl. "What is it?"

"A note someone sent to a PD."

You are not fit to live. I've decided that your life is going to be forfeited in payment for another's. He scanned the rest, a rambling tirade about truth and justice, then glanced at the signature, *Someone who cares.*

Lucas looked up at Dick. "Someone who cares? What in the hell is that supposed to mean?"

Dick shrugged. "Who knows? These sort of notes come in all the time, especially to PDs. It's part and parcel of their job, I'd think."

Lucas tossed the letter onto the desk and sank back in the chair. "Of course it is. They let the scum of the earth walk. It's a wonder they don't have to have a bomb squad follow them around." He squeezed the red ball over and over again. "If Jimmy Barnes had stayed in jail when he was arrested last year, he wouldn't have been on the street high on PCP with a bullet for me."

Dick sat back, lacing his fingers behind his head and looking at Lucas from under lowered lids. "Exactly. And there are people out there who aren't as pragmatic about it as you are. They actually get mad."

Lucas grimaced. "I sound bitter?"

"Just a bit."

He shook his head. "Yeah, I guess I do. It's just frustrating. A cop puts his life on the line and some solemn do-gooder finds a loophole and the perp walks."

"Jimmy Barnes didn't walk. He did a straight ten years."

Lucas looked at the paper he'd discarded on the desk. "What's this all got to do with me?"

Dick tapped a stack of papers near his elbow. "These are more letters just like the one you saw. Last week the letter writer escalated to leaving messages for the PD at the office. Then Ryan Sullivan, the assistant DA, called me yesterday morning and told me that the writer's made direct contact with the PD. Called an unlisted home number and threatened death."

"It sounds as if the PD's got trouble."

"Sure does. They're asking for our help."

"Tell them to get a bodyguard."

"We can't tell them that."

"Why?"

"Because there's a possibility that someone connected with the department's involved."

Lucas frowned. "How in the hell do you figure that?"

"Phrases in the letters and on the phone, they said that the perps have been getting off, that Mirandizing isn't good enough anymore, not when the PD works at finding loopholes."

Lucas sank back in the chair. "Anyone could use that language."

"Could, but it's not very probable. There's more to it than I can discuss with you."

"You think some cop's trying to throw the fear of God into the PD and going over the line doing it?"

"Possibly."

"Any ideas who?"

"None."

"Then what are you supposed to do?"

Dick sat forward, resting his elbows on the desk. "We're going to give the PD protection until we know what's going on for sure."

Lucas almost laughed at that. "Protection? What cop would want to spend twenty-four hours a day protecting someone who's out to undo everything they..." His voice trailed off as he suddenly understood. The medication must have dulled his thinking, or he would have zeroed in on this a long time back. "Oh, no, you don't. I want to *work,* not baby-sit some liberal, bleeding-heart PD."

"You said you wanted to work," Dick said, "and I need you on it. I want it kept quiet, but going through the department isn't always discreet. And we don't want this spread all over the papers."

Lucas shook his head. "You've got others—"

"No, I don't. It's the holiday season, and we're under a crunch. We need every man we can get on duty, and since you're going to be limited for a while, you're the logical choice. Besides, you don't have any family around here, and it wouldn't be so hard for you to get away for a week or so."

"What do you mean, get away?"

"We're trying to nail this as quickly as we can, and we need to keep the PD under tight surveillance. We figured getting the situation localized would be the best bet."

"Why don't you just spell it out in simple, direct English? Start with defining localized."

"We're going to put you a on cruise ship. Just look on this as a bonus. A cushy job, a cruise—and you can take a bit longer to heal." He almost smiled. "And don't thank me."

Lucas stopped squeezing the ball and stared right at Dick. "The department's footing the cost of a cruise to protect some PD from a loony who *might* be a cop?"

"Yes, and this comes straight down from the top, way up there. It's priority one, and you've volunteered for the job."

"Plain English, Dick."

"All right. We need her out of the way while we figure out who's doing this to her."

"Not for her protection, but to protect the department?"

"The PD gets protection, but that's just a bonus. We need to get whoever's behind the threats and do a hell of a lot of damage control."

Lucas could have almost laughed. "That sounds like a politician speaking to me."

"Good politics wouldn't hurt, and just think of the fallout if anything happens."

Lucas knew when he was cornered, especially if there was the possibility that this went beyond the department. At least he'd be working and not staring at four walls, he rationalized. "All right. I understand. Just tell me who it is I'm supposed to be going on this cruise to protect?"

"Shelley Kingston."

Lucas was on his feet before the full name was uttered and had to control the urge to throw the red ball right at Dick. "What the hell? Is this a joke?"

Dick rocked back in his chair, not letting Lucas's anger rile him at all. "Do I look like I'm joking?"

"I might be able to look past the work of some of the PDs, but that's one I can't."

"Lucas, you don't have to like a person to protect them. Hell, if that was a prerequisite, ninety percent of the city wouldn't have police protection."

"Yeah, and ninety percent of the city didn't get the charges against Freddy Monroe dropped because of inadmissible evidence. God, she got him off and in less than a week, he killed a *cop*." Lucas leaned forward, pressing his good hand flat on the desk, crushing the letters and not caring. "A *good* cop. Larry Hall shouldn't have died in that flophouse trying to bring in Monroe. And he wouldn't have if Kingston had left Monroe to rot in jail."

Dick didn't blink. "Are you done?"

Lucas exhaled harshly. "You went to the funeral."

"Larry knew his job, he knew the risks. We all do."

"It stinks," he muttered.

"What's going to stink is if we don't find out who's behind the threats and the crazy turns out to be some-one connected to the department. And I'm tired of doing this."

"Of doing what?"

"Of trying to talk people into doing what has to be done. It took me the best part of yesterday afternoon trying to talk Kingston into taking this cruise, and now you're giving me a royal pain. If someone offered me a cruise, I'd jump at it. I wouldn't care if I had to protect my mother-in-law."

"It's not exactly a vacation," Lucas pointed out.

"I know that. You're going to have to protect the lady and her child."

"There's a child?"

"A seven-year-old daughter."

This was going from bad to worse. Lucas had never been around children very much, not even his nieces and nephews. And if he thought of them at all, he knew he wasn't cut out to be anywhere in the vicinity of them. "Like I said before, I'm not a baby-sitter."

"All you have to do is do your job, and to make it a bit easier, we'll clear someone on the crew to help out with the child."

"What about the husband?"

"He's out of the picture. They're divorced, and he lives someplace on the East Coast."

Lucas looked down at the papers under his hand and caught the phrase, *your life is going to be forfeited.* He pulled his hand back and straightened up as he looked at Dick. "How long would I have to do this?"

"The cruise lasts for a week, then, with any luck, we'll have it all wrapped up."

Lucas raked his good hand through his dark hair. "All right. I can take anything for a week. What do you want me to do?"

Chapter Two

The next day all the details were arranged by the time Lucas walked back into Bentley's office.

"The ship sails at four this afternoon," Dick said. "You'll meet Kingston and the kid on board. We're going through the passenger list and we've got full cooperation from the crew on the ship. Your cabin's right next door to theirs." He looked under the papers on his desk and pulled out a beige envelope. "Here's everything you'll need, and there's a voucher in there for some cash. Get it before you leave."

Lucas took the envelope with his free hand. "And when I get back?"

"We'll see how you are and talk things over," Dick said.

Lucas nodded, then turned and started to leave. But as he got to the door, Dick said, "Lucas. One more thing."

He turned. "What's that?"

"Have a merry Christmas."

Lucas managed a slight smile. "Sure," he said, then left.

As he walked down the green-tiled corridor, past the interrogation rooms and the evidence room, he pushed the envelope into the pocket of his tweed jacket. At the elevators, he hit the button and when the doors slid open, he got in the empty car and headed down for the garage level.

But when he stepped out in the low-ceilinged concrete structure, he didn't head for his car. He walked toward the main entrance, up the ramp and out onto the street into the coolness of the December day. He turned right and went down two blocks to the old courthouse, took the front steps that ran up between massive concrete pillars two at a time and went through the open doors into the lobby.

He crossed the marble floor and scanned the schedule boards until he found Kingston on the docket and the courtroom she was in this morning. Second floor, in Judge Overton's court, room ten-zero-six. He was at least going to take a look at the woman before he met her on the ship later.

He took the elevator up and slipped into the courtroom, taking a seat in the last row by the door. Only a scattering of spectators was in the thirty-by-thirty-foot room. On the other side of the railing near the front was the judge's raised desk facing the spectator gallery, and two tables facing the judge, one for the prosecution on the right and one for the defense on the left. At the defense table sat a fat, totally bald man in a hot pink tank top with tattoos covering both arms.

Lucas didn't spare him more than a passing glance. The man was just like a hundred others Lucas had met on the street on the wrong end of a bust. What he no-

ticed was the blond woman with her back to the room
sitting by the man.

Right then the judge said, "Ms. Kingston?"

Lucas watched her sort through some papers, then
stand to face the judge. "Yes, Your Honor," she said
in a low, slightly husky voice.

Lucas took in her height, maybe five-seven or five-
eight, and almost boyish figure in a plain navy suit
worn with a white blouse. Golden hair was caught in
a simple twist secured by a silver clip. He couldn't tell
much else, but when she spoke in an even tone, he
rhythmically worked the red ball he had in his bad
hand.

"When my client, Mr. Garcia, was arrested, he'd
been stopped for expired tags on the car he was driving. The arresting officer allegedly found drugs under
the floor mat in the back on the passenger side. We
contend that when the officer searched the car, he had
no cause. My client was neither under the influence of
any illegal substance, nor was he resisting the officer
in any way. And there was no way that the arresting
officer could have known the drugs were there without a thorough search. Therefore, we ask that the
court drop the charges against my client because the
evidence was obtained in an illegal manner, and as
such is rendered inadmissible in this court."

Lucas watched the judge pick up a piece of paper
and scan it. Then he looked at the attorney at the other
table. "Mr. Talbot, you talked to the arresting officer?"

"Yes, Your Honor, but—"

"Is what Ms. Kingston contends true?"

"Your Honor, the arresting officer was well acquainted with Mr. Garcia from past arrests and he assumed—"

The judge shook his head and dropped the paper. "That's not good enough. I'm afraid I have no other recourse than to drop the charges against Mr. Garcia. Without evidence, there is no case." He looked at the defense table. "Ms. Kingston, there was apparently a good amount of drugs involved in this case. Maybe you can explain to your client that it would behoove him to never show his face in my courtroom again."

"Yes, Your Honor, I will," Shelley Kingston murmured.

The judge hit his gavel on the desk. "This court is in recess until one o'clock this afternoon."

Lucas felt distaste rise in his throat, and the pain in his shoulder and hand intensified as he clenched the red ball. Another lowlife on the streets. He watched as the tattooed man smiled slyly at a man sitting in the spectator chairs right behind him, then stood and, after saying something to his lawyer, took off.

He burst through the exit gate in the rail, met up with his friend, then they headed for the exit, slapping each other on the back and smiling. Lucas felt the urge to punch the expression off Garcia's face, but as the two men passed, he just stood and watched them leave. As the doors swung shut behind them, he stepped out into the aisle to leave. He'd seen enough.

Unexpectedly, something struck him in his left arm, and he barely bit back a gasp as pain radiated into his neck and shoulder. The ball flew out of his grasp on impact, and as he clutched at his arm, he spun around and saw Shelley Kingston crouched at his feet trying to pick up papers that had been scattered on the beige carpet when her briefcase had opened. He grimaced at the top of her head. It looked as if the damned briefcase had popped open, hitting him in the arm.

Then he looked around and saw the exercise ball by the gate in the railing. He hurried over to retrieve it, and when he had it, he turned to find Shelley Kingston just straightening up with her closed briefcase in her hands.

His first direct look at the woman stunned him. She was anything but boyish, with full breasts not entirely disguised by the straight cut of her jacket. True lavender eyes framed by lush lashes stared at him, and a touch of high color brushed exquisite cheekbones.

The woman wore little or no makeup, but she certainly didn't need it. Lucas wasn't facing the harridan he'd expected, and it took him off balance to find a woman who under any other circumstances would have attracted him. And oddly, he had the craziest idea that he'd seen her before. Maybe a news clipping or magazine piece? He couldn't begin to remember, yet the feeling of knowing her persisted.

"Sorry, I didn't see you," she said in a slightly breathless voice that played havoc with his nerves. "I was in a hurry."

As her gaze dropped to his hand that held the ball, he stilled the almost unconscious motion of squeezing the rubber. He hadn't meant to meet her, just watch her and see what he'd be up against for the next week. But here he was facing her, stunned by her looks and appalled at what she'd just accomplished before the judge and uneasy that he'd met her before.

"I didn't see you, either," he murmured.

Shelley stared at the man three feet from her. He was tall and dark, and his broad shoulders were defined by a gray tweed sports coat worn over a black T-shirt along with jeans and scuffed running shoes. As she met his dark gaze under straight eyebrows, she was hit by a certain maleness about him that was hard for her to define or assimilate.

She couldn't remember the last time she'd looked at a man in any other way than impersonally or as a client. But with an intensely scrutinizing expression on a roughly hewn face that seemed to be all angles and planes, he reminded her for a split second that she was a woman. Then she realized he was looking at her as if he thought he knew her, and that jarred her.

There was something about him that nudged at her memory, but it was elusive and too far back to grasp. Yet she knew if she'd ever met him, she would have remembered.

Before she could say anything else, he took a step toward her and said in a deep voice, "I don't know too many people who could get someone like that off scot-free. You did a good job, counselor."

The heavy sarcasm in his words cut through whatever madness the past moment had created, and in the next instant, Shelley felt apprehension slide up her spine. She'd been so caught up in the moment that she hadn't realized the courtroom was empty except for the two of them, and there was something edgy about this man.

He never stopped rhythmically squeezing a small red object in his hand. And his words... She felt her whole being tense. The tone was the same as the notes and the called threats, even if the voice wasn't familiar.

"I just practice law," she said, gripping her briefcase so she could swing it if she had to.

"Law? I guess the law really is blind. How do you live with yourself getting someone like Garcia off?"

She could see anger in his eyes, and Shelley mentally calculated the distance to the doors. If she screamed, would there be anyone outside to hear her? The building emptied quickly at lunchtime. She felt totally exposed and vulnerable, cursing the fact she'd rejected the suggestion that a bodyguard stay with her until she sailed on the cruise ship.

She'd thought she'd be safe in the courthouse, that people would be around, that familiar territory gave her an edge. But she knew she had no advantage right now. None at all. She'd stood up to some of the basest people in her job, facing down drug dealers, gang members, even murderers, but she was letting this stranger squeezing what looked like a simple red ball scare her.

"I just do my job," she said quickly, taking a half step back as she spoke.

"Some job," he muttered.

"What do you have to do with this case?" she asked.

"Nothing. I was just here to watch the law in action."

She was holding on to the briefcase so tightly, her hand was tingling. "The law has to work for everyone, or it doesn't work for anyone," she said, then made her move. "I have to go," she said as she turned and made herself walk, not run, toward the door.

When she reached out to touch the cool wood of the door, she heard the man say, "See you," and she didn't stop. She pushed the door open, stepped through and out into the deserted corridor. Her heart was beating faster than normal, and she had to kill the urge to look behind her to check and see if the man was following her.

Quickly, she started for the elevators. Even though she was forcing herself to just walk briskly, she was mentally running. When she pushed the down button, she chanced a look over her shoulder, but didn't see anyone. He hadn't followed her. A breath came more easily to her as the elevator doors slid back and she stepped into the car.

By the time the elevator started downward, Shelley could feel her heartbeat returning to a normal rhythm. Nothing happened. Nothing at all, except she'd let a stranger scare her to death. She gripped the briefcase and stared at the flashing floor numbers. Right now she had to get herself together, finish off the last of her work, pick up Emily from school and head down to the docks to meet the bodyguard who'd be with her for the next week.

LUCAS STARED at the courtroom doors as they swung shut after Shelley Kingston left, and didn't move until the doors stilled. Then he realized he was totally alone. He didn't have any idea why he confronted her like that. Worse, he didn't know why he felt a gut-level uneasiness about being around her for a week.

He felt the tension in him increasing, and with a low oath he headed for the doors. When he stepped out into the corridor, he didn't see anyone at all. As he looked at the elevators farther down to the left, he saw the doors just sliding shut and knew Shelley Kingston was gone. But at four o'clock, he'd meet her again.

He grimaced at the thought and started down the hall. This hadn't worked out at all. He'd meant to size her up, observe her without her ever knowing. But he'd blown it. When he got to the elevators, he pushed the down button and the doors on the end opened immediately. When he stepped inside and the doors slid shut, Lucas saw his reflection distorted by the polished metal.

He could see his hand working the ball, and he made himself stop and push the ball into his jacket pocket. It was almost an addiction for him, probably because it was the one thing he could do to counteract the impairment of his nerves from the bullet.

He met his gaze in the distorted metal and could see the dark frown on his face, evidence of the pain that was getting worse by the minute. But he wouldn't take any more of the painkillers the doctors had given him. No matter how much his arm hurt, he hated the foggy thinking more.

He massaged his aching arm with his good hand. Since he'd finally been put back to work, no matter what the assignment, he couldn't afford to dull his thought process or his reflexes with drugs. He had a sudden memory of Shelley Kingston with her lavender eyes and her chin lifted slightly as she met his sarcasm head-on.

Then it hit him. He knew where he'd seen her. And the curse that he uttered rang in the confines of the elevator. The funeral. The woman off to the side. Blond and pale. She'd been there.

As the elevator slid to a quiet stop and the doors started to open, Lucas watched his reflection sliding away. But it didn't disappear before he saw the grimace on his face.

But this time it wasn't from the physical pain in his body.

"MOMMY, it's so pretty and big, and it really floats," Emily said in awe as she bounced up and down on one of the two queen-size beds.

Shelley looked around the cabin. The blue and white color scheme was light and airy, and despite her suspicions that she'd get the leftovers since the arrangements had been made so late, they had a large cabin with a view.

When she'd contacted Captain Bentley to tell him about the man in the courtroom, she'd given up fighting his suggestion for protection until the ship sailed. He'd introduced her to Bernice Bonds, a policewoman who had brought them to the ship and settled them in. Bernice had mentioned an upgrade, but this was more than that.

This was almost elegant, with a private bath including a Jacuzzi and a walk-in closet big enough to set up house in. She wondered what strings Bentley pulled to get the accommodations on a day's notice.

"It's pretty, but if you keep bouncing on the bed you're going to get seasick," she told Emily.

Emily stopped, but wrinkled up her nose. "How does the sea get sick, Mommy?"

"It's *you* who gets sick, silly."

"How can I get sick by being on the bed?" Emily persisted with her unerring logic.

"It's not the bed," Shelley started, but was cut off by a knock on the cabin door.

She crossed and called through the barrier. "Who is it?"

"It's me, Bernice."

Shelley undid the chain and opened the door to Bernice, a slender woman of about thirty dressed casually in jeans and a denim jacket. "Good news. I got everything arranged," she said as she came into the room, "and look who I ran into wandering around the upper deck."

She motioned behind her, and Shelley turned to see a man coming into the cabin right after Bernice. She could almost feel her mouth dropping open in surprise when she recognized the man she'd bumped into in the courtroom. He'd changed into a chambray shirt, well-worn Levi's and the scuffed running shoes. And his sudden appearance made Shelley feel as if she'd been thrown into some perverted nightmare.

Before she could think of what to do, Bernice said, "This is Lucas Jordon, the lucky son of a gun who gets to be your bodyguard on this cruise."

Shelley stared at him, not sure if she was relieved he wasn't the person harassing her or furious that he'd baited her in the courtroom with words he had to know would scare her. One look in his dark-as-night eyes and she edged toward the furious. He obviously wasn't the least surprised to see her here, so he had to know who she was when he'd met her in the courtroom. He'd known all along.

"Ms. Kingston," he murmured as he held out his hand to her.

She felt Emily at her side, grabbing at her hand, and she ignored his hand, but she didn't look away from Lucas Jordon. "Are you going to explain what that was all about this morning?"

"I was just checking you out."

"You deliberately tried to scare me by saying those things to me."

"I didn't mean to scare you. I just said what I meant," he said without blinking.

Shelley cursed the heat that rose in her face, and she turned to Bernice. "This is not acceptable at all."

Bernice looked confused. "What isn't?"

"Him. This man being my bodyguard."

The woman shook her head. "Why?"

"He doesn't like me," she said, knowing as the words came out how absolutely juvenile they sounded.

Bernice looked at Lucas. "What's she talking about? I didn't think you even knew each other."

"We don't," he said. "But I ran into her this morning in Overton's courtroom."

"Then what in the—"

He shrugged, testing the fabric of the blue shirt. "Ask her."

Shelley felt more heat stain her cheeks, but she didn't back down. "He doesn't like what I do or what

I am. I don't think that makes for the best motivation to protect someone's life."

"Ms. Kingston, if liking what you are or what you do was a prerequisite for protecting you, you wouldn't have a chance in hell of finding a cop in this city who'd take the job."

Her cheeks were on fire now, but she stood toe-to-toe with the man. "Who made you judge and jury?"

"I'm just a cop who got roped into this." His control was infuriating. "I don't have a choice, not any more than you do now."

She looked at Bernice. "Can't you come with us, or get Bentley to find someone else?"

Bernice shook her head. "As inviting as this cruise would be, I'm heading home for Christmas. And I can save you a call to Bentley. He doesn't have anyone else who he can assign to you."

Shelley almost told Bernice to take Lucas Jordon and leave. She'd go this alone, but when Emily tightened her grip on Shelley's hand, she couldn't say the words. It wasn't just her in this. Emily had been pulled into it, too. She looked at Lucas. "Maybe you're a bit like me."

At least those words brought a reaction, a tugging of his dark eyebrows together over his eyes. "What are you talking about?"

"We both deal with people we don't like, but we do our job."

He shook his head. "I lock up most of the people I have to deal with. You let them go so you can go to their victims' funerals."

Shelley felt new shock ricochet through her. The funeral. That's where she'd seen him. Dark and alone by the police contingent. "That's not fair," she muttered.

Bernice stepped between the two of them with her hands raised. "Whoa. Time out. We aren't talking fair here. Lucas is here to protect you, and he'll do it. You're here to stay safe until they catch that psycho."

"What's a psycho?" Emily asked.

Shelley saw Lucas look at Emily, and that didn't help a thing. His frown only deepened, even though just looking at Emily could make the world right for Shelley. "Who're you?"

"Emily Sarah Kingston."

"Well, a psycho, Em—"

"Emily," the child said, enunciating it slowly and drawing it out as if she was talking to a person who was a bit slow. "My name is Emily."

He shrugged sharply. "Sure. Emily. A psycho is a crazy person who the police need to catch and lock up and make sure he stays that way."

"Like that one who's been bothering my mommy?"

"Exactly."

"And you're going to lock them up?"

"Until the psycho gets a lawyer like your mother and takes a hike."

"They get to go to the mountains?" Emily asked with pure seriousness.

Shelley could have laughed at Lucas's confused expression if she hadn't been so angry.

"The mountains?" Lucas asked.

Let him get out of this on his own, Shelley thought.

"Hiking, in the mountains," Emily explained. "Me and Mommy did that before. Do they really let bad people go hiking?"

He exhaled and glanced sharply at Shelley. "Some do, but not in the mountains. They just go hiking on the streets."

"But you can't hike—"

"Emily, that's enough," Shelley finally said. "We just have to let Mr. Jordon do his job and leave it at that."

"Then you get to do your job," Lucas muttered.

"You both get to do your jobs," Bernice said, cutting off any other conversation. "Let's agree to disagree and work on keeping everyone safe."

Shelley bit her lip to keep from saying anything else to Lucas. "You're right, Bernice. That's the most important thing."

"Are you staying in this cabin?" Emily asked Lucas.

Shelley felt her face heat up again, and she turned to look down at Emily. "Of course not, Emily. Mr. Jordon has his own cabin."

"And his cabin is right next door to yours," Bernice said as she crossed to a door in the side wall to the right. She turned the knob and opened the barrier to show another cabin done in the same blues and whites, but a bit smaller than the main cabin. "All you have to do is knock on his door and he's there, anytime, day or night."

Emily let go of Shelley to cross to the door and look inside. Then she turned. "It's nice, but not as pretty as ours. And it's only got one bed."

Lucas went past Shelley, leaving a hint of after-shave and maleness hanging in the air. She refused to breathe too deeply as he strode to the door, stepped past Emily and disappeared into his cabin. Without hesitating, Emily followed him inside.

Shelley could hear Emily talking, asking questions followed by the deep rumble of Lucas's voice touched with impatience. This time she did smile. He deserved her perpetual interrogation, at the least. Let a seven-year-old ask the questions that only she could think up. Maybe he could explain seasickness to her. And heaven help him if he called her Em again.

"I have to get going," Bernice said as she moved toward the door. "You have a lovely cruise and a safe one. They're doing a complete check on all the passengers you'll be near, and trust me—" She glanced at the open door to Lucas's cabin. "He's got a bad attitude, but he's really good at what he does. It's just that he's been off duty for a while, and cops always go through withdrawals when they can't work."

Shelley could understand that all too well. Sometimes she felt that her work would consume her if she didn't have Emily. "Why was he off duty?"

"He took a couple of bullets. The damn things shattered bones in his shoulder, but he's recovering."

Shelley couldn't remember if another cop had been wounded when Hall had been killed. She had no idea why it bothered her so much to think Lucas had been there, that the man she'd seen at the funeral was in pain because he could have seen another cop killed in front of his eyes.

The image of him at the cemetery in the gray mists, an image she carried in her mind with a disturbing clarity, came to her. And she understood his pain. Most of all, if he knew she was the one who had defended Freddy Monroe, she understood that raw anger in him when he looked at her.

Chapter Three

"He was involved in that shoot-out a few months ago?" Shelley managed to ask before Bernice left.

Bernice looked at Shelley, her expression tighter now, the smile gone. "One of the shoot-outs. But his ended up a bit better than another one. At least he wasn't killed the way the other cop was."

Somehow it made Shelley feel a bit better that Lucas wasn't part of the horror of the Hall killing. "He's all right now?"

"Still got problems, but he's a lot better." Bernice looked right at Shelley. "Believe me, he's a good cop. Give him a chance."

"I don't have a choice," Shelley said.

"Nope, you don't," Bernice said and the smile came back. "Have fun. I'll see you when you get back."

Shelley went to the door with her. "Thanks for all you've done."

"Merry Christmas. Ho, ho, ho, and all that."

"You, too."

As Bernice left with a wave, Shelley closed the door and put on the security bolt. Then she turned and crossed to the connecting door. She peeked inside at

Lucas unpacking his luggage into a dresser by the door. Emily was right beside him looking up at him.

"How come you've got a ball with you?" she asked.

"It's an exercise ball to help make my hand better." He put the red ball on the top of the dresser. "I use it a lot."

"What's that?" Emily was asking as Lucas took a stack of white clothes out of his suitcase he'd lain open on the bed.

"My underwear," he said as he pushed them into the top drawer.

"My mom's underwear is all colored and silky. Why are yours all white?"

"Men wear white," he muttered as he dumped some socks in the same drawer.

"Why?"

"Ask your father," Lucas said as he lifted some shirts out of his case.

"Can't."

He looked at the child. "Why not?"

"He's busy. He flies all over. He's been in Japan and Australia and London. And he's really busy making money, so I can't call him. It costs too much."

"I thought you said he was making money," Lucas said as he crossed to the closet and reached for hangers.

"He is, but my mom has a hard time making money. Public defenders don't make a lot, you know. So they have to econo...econim..."

"Economize," Lucas supplied as he began to put his shirts on the hangers one at a time.

"Yeah, that's it. So we can't use the phone too much, or the bill's a killer."

Lucas looked at Emily and actually smiled. "A killer, huh?"

"That's what Mom says."

Shelley felt a jolt seeing the man smile. The transformation was stunning. From dark and brooding, he went to... She couldn't find words that fit, but the closest she could come was human, and if she was honest, sexy.

"What else does your mom say?" Lucas asked.

"That money's tight and that the sea gets sick."

Lucas shook his head. "The sea gets sick?"

"Yeah, that's what she said, and she never lies. She says that lying should be a crime."

"What sort of lies?"

"I don't know." Emily went to the curtains and tugged them back to expose a round window that let in bright sunlight. "Maybe like Santa Claus."

"Santa Claus lies?"

Emily turned to Lucas, her tiny nose crinkled up. "Of course not."

"Everyone knows Santa's truthful."

"Mr. Jordon—"

"Lucas."

"Lucas, everyone knows that Santa isn't real, so he can't lie." She came closer to him. "You know that, don't you?"

He looked taken back. "How old are you?"

"Seven."

"I thought when kids were seven they believed in Santa Claus and the Easter bunny and the tooth fairy."

She shrugged her shoulders in an airy gesture. "Oh, some seven-year-olds do, but it's because their parents lie to them. My mom tells me the truth all the time. She told me they were just fairy tales that someone made up. She's the one who buys me my presents, but this year I have to get mostly clothes 'cause money's tight."

"Emily," Shelley said as she stepped into the room to break up the conversation. "We need to unpack."

Emily looked at Lucas. "We can talk some more later, all right?"

"I guess so," he said as Emily skipped out of the room.

Shelley looked at Lucas. "And we'll talk later."

"We'll talk now," he said. "We need to set down ground rules so we won't step on each other's toes too much."

"You're right." She looked through the connecting door and saw Emily with her suitcase open on the bed. "Honey, get unpacked while I talk with Mr. Jordon."

Emily looked up. "Are you mad at him?"

She thought she was well past mad. "Why would you say that?"

"You look mad," she said.

"You just unpack and no matter what, don't answer the phone or the door. You call me if anyone comes to the cabin or calls." When she saw the look that Emily was going to ask more questions, she said,

"You know what's going on. You do as I say. Do you understand?"

"Yes, Mommy."

"Now, I have to talk to Mr. Jordon and get something settled before we go on this trip. I'll be right back," she said and closed the door.

As she turned to find Lucas a few feet from her, she knew that closing the door had been a major mistake. All it had accomplished was to shrink the room, a room already filled with this man's presence. "Rules?" she asked, crossing her arms over her breasts. She knew it was a defensive stance, but right now all she wanted to do was to get this over with. "What are they?"

Lucas came a step closer, effectively eliminating some of the barrier of space she only wished she could widen. But she stood her ground. "First, you do nothing, absolutely nothing, without telling me first."

She nodded silently.

He tucked his fingertips in the pockets of his jeans and rocked forward on the balls of his feet. The space grew even smaller. "Second, you're to keep to yourself as much as possible on this cruise. If you meet anyone, get their names, and I'll check the list for them. Third, the child is not to go with anyone I haven't approved of. Fourth, don't tell anyone why you're really here, I don't care how nice they seem or how they ask or what they ask. You're on a vacation for the holidays. Period."

She stared at him, not having any trouble seeing the hard-edged cop in him. She just wished she could ignore the fact that he was so disturbingly male. But she knew that would be like trying to ignore a hurricane. "Do I get a written list?"

He ignored her sarcasm by asking his own question. "Do you understand the rules?"

"Of course I do. I have a decent grasp of the English language and I can comprehend abstract concepts."

He exhaled harshly. "You don't have to like them, you just have to follow them."

She shrugged. "Is that everything?"

"For now."

"Good," she muttered and turned to make her escape, but he stopped her when he spoke up.

"Oh, there is one more thing, Ms. Kingston."

She didn't turn as she asked, "What, Mr. Jordon?"

"The child—"

She threw him a slanting glance over her shoulder. "Her name is Emily."

She didn't expect him to smile, but he did, a lifting at the corners of his mouth that eased some of the harshness. "So I was told. Emily." The smile died, and Shelley almost hated its disappearance. "I'm not a baby-sitter. Bentley said that he'd contacted the main offices for the line and they had someone who could help with the—with Emily. They've cleared her. After you get settled in, knock on the door and I'll go and find her."

Without a word, Shelley left, and once she was in her own cabin with the door shut behind her, she finally took a deep breath.

"Mom, does Lucas know a lot of psychos?"

Shelley looked at her daughter by the bed, her clothes still in the open suitcase. At least she didn't ask if Lucas *was* a psycho. "I'm sure he does, since he's a policeman. Now, why haven't you unpacked?"

"I didn't know if we were staying."

"Why would you say that?"

"You said you had to get things settled before we can go on this trip."

"I didn't mean that going on the trip depended on that." She crossed to the bed and sank down on the edge to look at Emily. "Listen to me, sweetheart. We're going on this boat, and we're going to have a good time, no matter why we had to come."

"But you don't like boats."

Shelley didn't have a clue when she'd ever said that to Emily, but the truth was she didn't like water. She hated it. "I like *this* boat."

"Good," Emily sighed. "I was afraid you'd be mad at Lucas and we'd have to go back home."

"No, we aren't going back home, not until the police have a chance to see if they can find the person making those calls." She reached out and pulled Emily into a hug. "For now, we're safe, and we're going to have fun."

Emily snuggled into her. "That sounds good."

Shelley held Emily back to look her in the face. "But you have to smile. That's a rule."

"Oh, Mommy."

"Come on. Smile, or we don't go."

Emily fought the expression, her lips twitching with humor that she could barely contain. "I don't have to," she said.

"Oh, yes, you do, and I'll help you." Shelley knew just where to tickle Emily for the best results, and she barely had to touch her on her ribs before the child let out a loud shriek.

She grabbed at her mother's hands, and the two of them fell backward onto the bed. As the suitcase slipped off onto the floor, Emily screamed, "Stop! Please, no!" between bursts of uncontrollable screeching. "Please," she gasped as they rolled on the bed, tangling with the spread. "Please, stop!"

The sound of a door crashing against the wall startled Shelley, and as she twisted toward the sound with Emily caught in her arms, she saw Lucas in the door. He was dressed only in his jeans, his shirt discarded to expose a tanned chest with a sprinkling of dark hair. He held his gun with both hands, the barrel leveled at the two of them.

For a moment he looked confused, then demanded, "What in the hell's going on?"

Shelley scrambled up, tugging Emily with her until they were both sitting in the middle of the tangled bedspread. The suitcase had tumbled to the carpet, scattering the clothes, but Shelley didn't take her eyes off Lucas and the gun.

"Put that gun away," she breathed in a tight voice.

He acted as if she hadn't said a thing. "Who screamed?"

"We were playing," she said and felt Emily move closer to her side, peeking cautiously around her at the man with the gun. "Please," she said, "get rid of the gun."

Finally, he slowly lowered the gun to his side. "Don't ever do that again," he said in a low, tense voice.

Emily tugged at Shelley's arm. "Mommy, what's wrong?"

Shelley covered Emily's hand with hers, but didn't look away from Lucas. "It's a mistake, sweetheart. Mr. Jordon thought someone was hurting you. He didn't know we were playing."

"You were tickling me," Emily said.

"Yes, I was." She looked at Emily, whose eyes were still overly wide. "Pick up the clothes while I explain something to Mr. Jordon."

"He's mad, isn't he?"

"He's not the only one," Shelley muttered as she got off the bed and stood. "Now pick up your clothes." She looked at Lucas near the open door. "Your cabin?"

Without a word, he turned from her and went inside and she followed, then closed the door. The bed was mussed and Shelley had the idea that Lucas had been laying on the bed when he'd lunged for the door with the gun in his hand.

Right now he was at the windows where the curtains had been pulled back, and the setting sun was invading the cabin with deep colors, silhouetting his frame with the hues. She watched him tuck the gun in the waistband at the back of his jeans before he turned to look at her.

"I've got my own rules, Mr. Jordon," she said before he could say anything. "The number-one rule is that you're to *never* bring that gun out around Emily again. Do you understand?''

Lucas came toward Shelley, stopping just a few feet from her, and with him this close she could see that a sheen of moisture covered his skin and his expression looked strained. "I thought the kid was being killed," he bit out as he rubbed at his shoulder.

That was when she saw the scar, a knot of healing tissue that looked as if the cap of his shoulder had been torn off and reattached. Her thoughts faltered, and the anger she'd been containing seemed to dissipate until she found she was having trouble holding onto it. "We...we were playing," she managed to say and tried not to look at the damage to the man's skin.

He ran his hand roughly over his face and exhaled with a hiss. "You could have fooled me."

"I guess we did," she said without thinking.

He stared at her for a long moment, his expression tight, and it suddenly struck her that it wasn't from anger. The man was in real pain. "Just don't do it again," he muttered.

"Are you all right?" she asked.

He looked startled by the question. "It was a mistake."

"No, I meant, you . . . you look as if you don't feel very well."

"I moved too fast." He started to flex his shoulder, but stopped as the film of moisture on his skin increased.

Shelley bit her lip as the sight of the man naked from the waist up made her mouth go dry. He was lean, and each muscle was etched under the tanned skin. Averting her eyes from the scar, all she succeeded in doing was to glance at his chest, at the suggestion of dark hair that tapered down to the waistband of his jeans.

She jerked her eyes up to meet his dark gaze, and for a flashing second, she had the most horrible idea that he knew exactly where her thoughts had threatened to go. She spoke quickly to distract herself. "Bernice told me you were injured a few months ago."

"Two weeks before Larry Hall was killed," he snapped.

She hated the feeling of wanting to apologize to this man, to tell him she had no idea what was going to happen with Monroe, that she only did what she had to do. "You were shot?"

"A dumdum bullet ripped up my shoulder and damaged some nerves." He lifted his left hand palm up and stared at his fingers as he flexed them. "They had to operate, and they thought for a while they might have to amputate, but they didn't. It's going to take time to get back the full use, if I ever do."

"It's painful?"

He looked at her from under the shadow of his lashes, and the look only intensified whatever happened when this man was around her. "On an agony scale of one to ten, I'm down to a five on a day-to-day basis, some days a six. Right now it's topping out at eight."

She murmured something about being sorry, but all she could think of was the reaction she'd had in the courtroom to Lucas. Now it seemed that it hadn't stopped there. This man made her uncomfortable in such a basic way all she really knew right then was she wanted out of this room.

She touched her tongue to her lips. "I have to get back to Emily, but I just wanted to make sure you understood about the gun. Emily's not used to violence."

He came toward her as his expression tightened. "With the business you're in, how can you keep it from her?"

She could feel herself bracing as he got within a few feet of her. "She knows what I do. I've explained that, but that doesn't mean she's going to sit in court and spy on me."

He had the decency to look a bit taken aback by her statement. "I saw you at the funeral."

"I know."

He flexed his shoulder slowly as his fingers massaged the skin around the healed scar. "I was discharged from the hospital to be there."

"It was a terrible tragedy," she said, knowing the understatement of those words.

He stared at her for a long, intense moment, then moved abruptly to pass her and cross to a bar built in by the hall door to the suite. "A drink?"

"No, thanks." She stared at his bare back, at the way his muscles flexed as he moved, and she inched toward the connecting door. As she reached for the latch, Lucas turned with a bottle of water in his hand.

"I'll unpack, then we can find the woman who's going to help with Emily," she said as she gripped the door latch.

"Yeah, then we'll get something to eat. We were asked to sit at the captain's table for dinner, but I don't think that's wise. We need to keep a low profile, so we were assigned to a communal table for meals. *If* we go up for meals."

"What about you and me? Are we suppose to know each other?" No one had explained this part of the plan.

He shrugged. "We met when we were boarding and happen to be in cabins next to each other. We'll make up the rest as we go along."

"I'm not good at pretending," she said.

"I know, lying should be a crime. So should a lot of other things that aren't. Just keep it simple and casual, and let me take the lead."

She wondered if anything about this man was casual. "All right. I'll get Emily."

"And I'll get dressed."

When Shelley pulled the door open, she almost ran into her daughter who was rushing to the door. "Mommy, Mommy," Emily said in a breathless whisper. "Someone's trying to get into our room."

"What?"

"They knocked real soft once, now they're jiggling the handle."

Before Shelley could say anything else, Lucas moved to where she and Emily stood and held a finger to his lips, then whispered, "Get into the closet back there." He pointed behind him toward his bathroom. "Get inside and keep quiet, and stay there until I tell you to come out."

Shelley grabbed Emily by her hand and took her to the open closet, then urged Emily inside. Touching her cheek, she whispered, "Stay right here and be really quiet. No matter what happens, you stay in here. Okay?"

"Mommy, I—"

Shelley spoke quickly, "Emily, please, just do this for me. It's really important."

"Okay," she whispered.

She hated seeing her child so bothered, but she couldn't help that right now. She gave her a hug, then stood and eased the door closed. Quickly she crossed to Lucas.

He motioned her to get behind him, then he slowly withdrew his gun from his waistband. He reached for the handle with his free hand and opened the door, easing it silently back. Keeping the gun out of sight behind the barrier, he peered out into the hallway in the direction of her cabin.

Lucas knew he'd been off the job too long. His heart was pounding, and his hand on the doorknob felt damp. Even when he'd been facing the wrong end of a gun in the past, he hadn't felt this painful surge of adrenaline. As he moved to look down the corridor, he kept the gun behind the door.

A woman he'd never seen before was at Shelley's door fiddling with the lock. She wasn't in the uniform that the crew on the ship wore, but she was dressed all in white, in leggings and an oversize shirt that emphasized a large figure.

"Is there a problem?" he asked.

She darted him a quick look. "What?"

Lucas met the gaze of narrow eyes set in a plain face with broad features framed by extremely short black hair. "Do you need some help?"

"The key won't work," she said as she tugged a key out of the lock and held it up.

"You've got the wrong cabin."

She looked at the number. "No, that's not it. I've got the right cabin."

He tightened his grip on the gun. "I know who's in that cabin, and they didn't mention anyone else being with them."

She cocked her head to one side. "Who are you?"

"Who are *you?*"

She eyed him for a moment, then her expression softened with the suggestion of a smile. "Martha Webb."

Lucas felt almost dizzy with relief, and the tension in him began to dissipate. "Martha Webb," he repeated, recognizing the name of the woman Bentley had told him would meet them on board.

He pushed the door farther open and looked at Shelley. The instant he saw the apprehension in her expression he had a partial answer to why he had reacted so intensely to a threat that at best should have been considered minimal. He was afraid for her. Despite everything, there was something vulnerable in her, and he was afraid of anything harming her. He reasoned it was his job, but he knew it went beyond that. He just didn't know why.

"It's Martha Webb," he said.

She shook her head. "Who?"

"She's the one Bentley arranged to help with Emily."

She exhaled a shaky breath, and Lucas had to turn from the sight of her. Whatever was going on, he was having a hard time making himself not go and touch her and tell her that it was all right, that he was here to protect her and he'd do that very thing. He looked into the hall and spoke to Martha. "Wait right there."

He went into the cabin, pushed his gun into his waistband and turned to Shelley, who was at the closet getting Emily out. Talk about overreacting. He'd told her to put the child in a closet, for heaven's sake.

"It's all right, sweetheart," Shelley was saying. "It was a false alarm."

He watched Shelley hug the child, then take her hand and walk with her to where he stood. "You know the woman?" she asked.

"I haven't met her, but Bentley told me about her." He motioned to her cabin and led the way. "Come on and meet her for yourself."

"Lucas?" Emily said.

He glanced at her as they stepped into the next cabin. "What?"

"Who're we meeting?"

"The lady who's going to take you to the pool and to see the ship and to make sure you're safe when your Mom or I aren't around."

"Then why were you so scared?"

Lucas stared at the child. "Me?"

"You were scared, and so was Mommy. I was a bit, too."

"We weren't sure who it was," he said. "Your mom told you I'm here to make sure you're both all right. That's my job."

"Where's your gun?" the child asked with wide eyes.

"Why do you want to know?"

Emily looked up at him. "You might need to shoot the psycho if he tries to get us."

Chapter Four

Emily's words were said with innocent simplicity, but they struck Lucas hard. "I'm not going to shoot anyone," he said quickly and turned to head for the door. "Right now there's a lady standing out in the hallway waiting for us to answer the door."

When he opened the door, he faced Martha Webb. She seemed concerned. "Is everything all right in there?"

"Just great," Lucas murmured.

Emily came to stand by him. "I'm Emily."

Martha smiled as she held out her hand to the child. "Nice to meet you, Emily."

"Nice to meet you, too," Emily said politely.

"I can tell we're going to be great friends." Martha looked past the child. "And you must be Mrs. Kingston."

Shelley smiled at the woman, and Lucas wondered what it would be like to be the reason for putting a smile on the lady's face. "I'm Shelley."

"Dick Bentley told me all about you. He's a friend of my father's. I sent him my qualifications. He said he'd get them to you as soon as he could. Would you like me to get them now?''

Shelley trusted the woman and trusted Dick Bentley. "You can bring them to me later.''

Martha spoke to Emily. "Why don't you go and get changed into your swimsuit and we'll go up and take a look around for a while? Maybe we can take a little swim, if it's okay with your mother. Then we can look around the ship and figure out what you want to do for fun.''

Emily looked as if she'd been given a present. "Oh, yes, that sounds great.'' She turned to Shelley. "Is it okay, Mommy?''

"Sure. Go and get changed.''

The child didn't waste time running to the dresser, taking out something bright pink, then hurrying to the bathroom.

"Emily?'' Martha called after her. "Bring some sun lotion and a towel.''

"Sure thing,'' she said and went into the bathroom.

Once the door was closed, Martha looked at Shelley. "She's a real beauty. Looks a lot like you.''

"Thanks.''

"How are her swimming skills?''

"Like a fish in water.''

"Good. I'll take her up to the pools and give you two time to talk things over. I don't think we should be discussing this in front of her.''

"She knows what's going on. So don't worry about talking in front of her.''

Martha frowned. "She should know enough to watch what she's doing. You're right there. How old is she?"

"Seven."

"A lovely child," she murmured. "It's a shame that someone so important to you has been pulled into this ugly mess."

"What do you know about it?" Lucas asked.

Martha glanced at him. "Captain Bentley filled me in. He thought it best in order to protect the child."

He couldn't fight that logic at all. "How did you get this job?"

"As I said, Captain Bentley knows my father, and I've met him a few times. When he was going over the crew list, he recognized my name and called. I wasn't scheduled for this particular cruise, but my boss said I could do it on my own time and have full access to the facilities. And it wouldn't cost me a thing. How could I refuse?"

Bentley thought of everything. "What do you usually do on a cruise?"

"I'm in housekeeping, but I've helped with the children's activities before." She looked at Shelley. "Why don't you tell me what you've got planned, and I'll work out a schedule for Emily that'll fit into it."

"I haven't had time to really get settled in."

"Why don't you do that, and I'll take Emily for..." She looked at her watch. "For two hours. You're in the second seating for dinner, so I'll have her back in plenty of time to get changed."

"That sounds fine," Lucas said, then asked the question that had been bothering him. "The key, why did you have it?"

She looked at the key in her hand. "It's a pass key. I didn't know if you were on board yet, so I came down to see. When I knocked, no one answered, so I thought I'd come down and wait. I guess I picked up the wrong key for this area." She pushed it in a side pocket and shrugged with a smile. "I guess I didn't need it anyway."

Right then Emily burst out of the bathroom and went directly to Martha. She'd changed into a pink bathing suit with ruffles at the bottom and she was carrying a tube of lotion and a towel in her hands. "I'm all ready."

Martha glanced at Shelley. "We'll see you back here in two hours?"

"That's fine. And thanks so much for helping out."

"My pleasure," Martha said and opened the door. "Come on, kiddo, let's get this show on the road."

The last thing Lucas saw was Emily smiling at Martha and the woman taking the child's hand before the door closed. Then Lucas was alone with Shelley and he murmured, "At least that's settled."

"She seems to be nice," Shelley said, but she was frowning at the closed door.

"But?"

She looked at Lucas. "This situation has made me into a nervous mother. I'm worried about the safety of my child, and I worry when she's out of my sight, especially with what's going on."

"I can understand that."

She looked at him, the lavender of her eyes deep and rich. "Can you?"

It wasn't the child's safety that made him nervous. But her mother could make his heart pound. He turned from Shelley and crossed to the connecting door. "Yes, I can," he said. "I want people to be safe in this world, so I do my job and try to make a difference."

"Do I hear a but in that statement?" Shelley asked.

He faced her across the room, a woman of beauty who could make his heart race and an attorney who could make his blood run cold. "I do my job. You do yours. But we just nullify each other's efforts, don't we?"

"No, we complement them."

"Excuse me?"

She crossed the room to where he stood, infusing the air he breathed with the delicate fragrance that seemed to be part of her. "You protect people. So do I."

"You get people off."

"I protect the rights they have under the constitution."

He'd heard words like this often enough to hate them. "What about getting off someone you know sure as hell is guilty? That happens, doesn't it?"

Color touched her cheeks and emphasized her porcelainlike skin. "It could."

"That guy with the tattoos was lily white?"

"The arrest was messed up, not my argument. I didn't make the arresting officer do a faulty search and seizure. If he gets Garcia, he'd better get him with a clean arrest.''

"The letter of the law?''

"Absolutely.''

"And justice is blind?''

She lifted one finely arched eyebrow. "And it doesn't respect people, either.''

"Obviously. How else could you be around people like you deal with?''

"The same way you deal with the people you have to deal with.''

He stared at Shelley. He knew why he disliked what she did, and he knew that never in a million years could he accept it, but that didn't kill the fact that if he had to go to court, he wouldn't mind having her on his side. Contrary to his usual inclination for arguing something out to the bitter end, he actually backed off with one parting shot. "There's a big difference between an exterminator and a breeder.''

Her cheeks flamed. "That's a ridiculous thing to say.''

"Yes, it is, isn't it?'' he said as he turned from her and walked into his cabin. He said, "If you need anything, knock, and don't go anywhere without telling me,'' over his shoulder, then grabbed the door and swung it shut without looking back.

He hadn't taken more than two steps before a knock sounded on the connecting door. He stopped, waited, and when it happened again, he went to open the door. Shelley was there right in front of him. A frown cut between her lavender eyes.

"What is it?''

"A question."

"What?"

"I thought I was on this cruise to be out of reach of the nut who's harassing me."

"That's the idea."

"Then why did you react like that with the gun when Emily said someone was trying to get into our room?"

He eyed her. "Why did you tell Emily not to answer the door or answer the phone?"

"It was a precaution, but—"

"Exactly. A precaution. We hope that no one knows you're here, that you're on this cruise, but we can't depend on that. That's why I'm here. Does that explain things?"

"I guess so," she said.

"But?"

"Nothing." She shook her head, then met his gaze directly, and for a moment he thought he saw a glint of laughter deep in the lavender. "A breeder?"

He found a certain sense of shared humor an uneasy emotion for him with this woman after everything that had happened. "A bad choice of words," he murmured.

"A very bad choice," she said and turned away from him.

He closed the door quickly and headed right for the bathroom, pausing only long enough to pick up the red ball from the dresser. But the phone rang before he got to the bathroom, and he crossed to pick it up by the bed. "Yes?"

"Lucas? It's Dick Bentley."

"Hey, what's up?"

"That's just what I was going to ask you. How's it going?"

Lucas exhaled and squeezed the ball so tightly he felt the tendons in his arm protest. "It's barely started."

"Are you getting settled in?"

"Sure."

"But?" Bentley prodded.

"You know this wasn't what I had in mind when I asked you to let me get back to work. I can't believe you have me protecting this woman."

"On a nice, relaxing cruise where all you have to do is keep your eyes on the lady."

"Did you want anything else?"

"We're still working on the check for the passengers. I'll get it to you as quickly as possible."

"Martha Webb's here."

"Good. That should make things easier for you."

"Sure," Lucas said, then hung up and headed for the bathroom.

He went in, turned on the shower, and as steam filled the room, he looked at himself in the mirror that lined the wall. The reflection was a grim one, his face drawn into a tight frown, and the scar on his shoulder seemed more vivid than normal.

There was no way anything, including the presence of Martha Webb, was going to make this cruise any easier for him. His grip on the ball tightened until his shoulder felt fiery and his hand ached. Then he closed his eyes and understood the cause of the building tension in him.

Shelley's image filled his mind, and he opened his eyes quickly. With a raw oath, he threw the ball into the empty cabin, absorbed the searing pain it cost him, and heard it ricochet twice before it stilled.

SHELLEY UNPACKED and straightened the room for almost two hours, then changed her clothes. When she couldn't stand the silence anymore, she got up and crossed to the connecting door. Her hand hovered near the knob before she took a deep breath, then rapped on the door. There was only silence from inside, then suddenly the door clicked and Lucas stood in front of her.

The man was transformed from the rough-hewn cop in casual clothes to a darkly intense man in a well-cut navy sports jacket worn with gray slacks and a black turtleneck shirt.

She must have been staring because she saw his eyes narrow and his lips twitch. "Do I clean up well?" he asked.

She shifted a bit nervously, more than aware of the simple plainness of her dress. The blue chiffon had been her only *good* dress for the past few years. It had a simple scooped neckline, a tapered waist and full skirt that brushed her legs at the knees. For a moment she knew what a peahen must feel like next to a peacock. Lucas had all the flare. She was simply there.

"Very well. I was just wondering if this is dressy enough," she murmured.

As his eyes skimmed over her, she wished she hadn't said anything. Just the touch of his gaze made her body tingle, and she found herself fighting the urge to step back to put more distance between them. Then he murmured, "No one would take you for a PD in that dress."

Before she could say anything, he looked past her into the cabin. "Did Martha bring Emily back yet?"

"No. But she should be here pretty soon."

Right then a knock sounded on the cabin door, and Shelley was glad to turn and cross to it. Lucas was right behind her, and his hand covered hers as she reached out for the knob. When she turned, she was inches from him, so close she could feel the heat of his breath on her skin.

"*Never* open it without asking who it is," he whispered harshly, and his hand on her tightened, hovering just this side of real pain.

She wanted to jerk free, but made herself stay very still. "I was going to ask," she whispered.

Suddenly his hold on her was gone and he motioned to the door with his head. She leaned toward the barrier and asked, "Who is it?"

"Martha and Emily."

Shelley looked at Lucas and saw his right hand slowly coming out of the inside of his jacket. The gun. "Go ahead," he said softly.

When she opened the door, Emily burst into the room, her face wreathed in smiles. She ran to the closest bed and threw something on the spread, then turned to Shelley, her face lit with pleasure. "Mommy, you'll never, never, never guess what they let kids do."

Seeing Emily this happy seemed to balance out all the other things going on in Shelley's world. "What do they let kids do?"

"Gamble!" Emily squealed. "Can you believe it?"

"No, I can't," she said, looking at Martha as the woman stepped into the cabin.

The woman smiled indulgently at Emily. "They have tables for the children and they give them choc- olate candies that look like money to make their bets. The kids love it."

"*I* love it, and I won," Emily said, clapping her hands.

Shelley looked at the bed and saw a pile of bright foil-wrapped candy scattered on the blue spread. "That's your haul?"

"Yeah, fifty-two of them!" She tugged something out of her pocket and held up a large sucker. "The man dressed like Santa Claus gave me this and he said that he knew I'd been good. I asked him how he'd know that, because he didn't know me, but he just laughed."

"She's quite a realist, isn't she?" Martha asked.

"She knows what's real and what isn't," Shelley said.

"So, what games did you play?" Lucas asked Em- ily.

"Fish and the wheel! I went fishing and got a six and I got another one. And the ball got on the right number on the wheel. I won." The laughter died as Emily sank down on the bed and dropped the sucker on the spread before pressing a hand to her stomach. "I ate some of the candy, too."

"She had a hot dog and lemonade first." Martha went across to Emily and sank down on the bed by her, then looked at Shelley. "Why don't you two just go on up for dinner? I don't think Emily's very hungry, so I'll stay here with her until you come back."

Shelley crossed to her daughter and crouched in front of her. "Will you be all right, honey?"

Emily scrunched up her face. "My tummy feels funny."

"I'll call for some ginger ale and toast for her. That always fixes people right up," Martha said as she patted Emily's back and looked at Shelley. "Now, don't you worry. You two go on, have fun, and we'll be safe and sound in here. If we need you, we can have you paged."

Shelley glanced at Lucas, who seemed to be studying her intently. "What do you think?" she asked him. "Should we just stay down here tonight?"

"I think we need to look around, to get a feeling for the setup. If Martha's going to stay with the child, I think we should go up for a while. We don't have to stay long."

Shelley looked at Emily again and tipped her face up with her fingers on her chin. "You do what Martha tells you to do, and don't leave this room. All right?"

Emily nodded, then Shelley looked at Martha. "You sure this won't be a bother for you?"

"No, of course not. We'll be fine."

Shelley glanced at Lucas. "How do we do this?"

"You go up first, get settled at the table, and I'll be up in ten minutes."

For some reason she'd thought they were going together, and the idea of going alone made her feel vulnerable. "Are you sure that's necessary?"

He met her gaze. "Absolutely. Just remember the story that we met down here when we boarded."

"I think I can do that," she murmured and bent to drop a kiss on Emily's forehead. "Take care, honey, and I'll be back in a while. If you need me, you have me paged."

Lucas watched Shelley kiss the child, then with a glance at him, she headed for the door. The dress she'd thought was plain was anything but plain on her. It clung to the curves of her hips and flowed elegantly around legs that were surprisingly long and shapely. When he looked away as the door shut behind Shelley, he found Martha smiling at him.

She stood with a touch on Emily's head. "Well, you've got a very interesting evening ahead of you. And so do we." She looked at the child. "Come on," she said, "I'll help you get changed into your pajamas, then we'll get you something for your tummy."

"We'll be back in an hour or so," Lucas murmured and went into his cabin. He stood in the silence for all of a minute, considering giving Shelley more time to get settled at the table. But the idea of her being out there alone took that option away, and he headed for the door.

SHELLEY STEPPED into the main dining room of the ship and surveyed the room. It was built in three levels. In the center, at the lowest point, was a hardwood dance floor with a huge, thirty-foot Christmas tree decorated with crystal ornaments and twinkling lights. A scattering of couples danced near it to the strains of a small band at the back of the large room.

The other two levels rose up from the center, surrounding the dance floor with brass rails wrapped with garlands and holly. The room was a blur of deep reds and golds, garish by any standards, but with the softening effect of the massive chandeliers and the Christmas lights, it was lovely.

She scanned the domed ceiling, then stepped down shallow carpeted stairs to the lower levels. The numbers for the tables were discreetly displayed against silver vases holding brilliant poinsettias, and she finally spotted her table assignment off to the left, one level above the dance floor.

She approached the large round table that had been draped in lace and set with crystal and silver. Several people were already seated, and three chairs were empty. Any other time she would have smiled, said hello and sat down. But she felt guarded as she looked at the people sitting there, looking at her, waiting for her to take her seat.

Two elderly ladies were closest to her. It was obvious they were twins. Identical in appearance, from curly gray hair to brown eyes, rimless glasses and full-bosomed figures, they both looked up and smiled at her. "Oh, someone new," the woman closest to her said.

"Sit, make yourself comfortable," the other woman said in an identical tone.

As she pulled out the chair and settled on the plush red velvet seat, the first woman said, "We were waiting for everyone to get here before we all introduced ourselves." She looked at the two empty chairs. "I guess our last two dinner partners are going to be late, so why don't we introduce ourselves now and tell everyone a little bit about ourselves?" She smiled at the table at large. "I'm Jessie Warden and this is my sister, Lillian. We're retired teachers from Palo Alto and this is our first cruise." After having her say, she looked at a gentleman sitting by her sister. "And you, sir?"

The middle-aged gentleman by Lillian had grayish red hair, a luxurious salt and pepper mustache and pale blue eyes behind horn-rimmed glasses. "Lawrence Washburn," he said.

"And?" Jessie prodded.

"Professor of mathematics at the university. I'm on vacation."

"Lovely," Jessie murmured and went on to a couple next to him. "And you two?"

The man and woman were about thirty and had the look of very upscale yuppies. The man, a narrow-faced person with long dark hair, glanced around the table and mumbled, "Rory and Diane Lewis. We're on our honeymoon and we're from San Francisco."

Lillian beamed at them. "How lovely. How lovely."

Jessie cut right in as she motioned to the next gentleman. "And you, sir?"

"James Sloan," the man said in a gravelly voice. Wiry and tall, he could have been anywhere from forty to sixty, with dark eyes, rough skin and a smile that only touched his lips. "On vacation."

Right next to him was a blond man with a deep tan set off by a white dinner jacket. Hazel eyes were framed by pale lashes, and his full mouth curved in a brilliant smile. He spoke before Jessie could prompt him. "Brant Weston. Mill Valley. Single. Vacationing. Banking." He cast Jessie a slanted look. "Did I forget anything?"

Shelley heard the touch of sarcasm in his voice, but Jessie obviously didn't. "No, nothing." Then she looked at Shelley. "And you, my dear?"

"Shelley Kingston." Shelley shifted to let the waiter set a shrimp cocktail in front of her, then she reached for her wine goblet. Some of the cool condensation from the chilled white wine dampened the tips of her fingers. "I'm taking a break from work, and I live in San Francisco."

"You didn't say what you do for a living," Jessie said.

"I'm an attorney."

Brant let out a low whistle. "If I had an attorney like you, I'd make sure I got into trouble a lot more often."

The professor shook his head, and Jessie looked at Shelley. "An attorney? Oh, my, that's exciting."

"About as exciting as dealing with garbage, I'd bet," James Sloan said.

Shelley glanced at him. "Excuse me?"

"That's who needs a lawyer, the garbage of this world, unless you're one of those fancy lawyers who gets into litigation and that sort of thing."

Shelley felt her stomach tighten at his tone and wished Lucas had come up with her. "I help people who need help," she murmured.

"And I bet you're just terrific at it," Sloan muttered.

"It's a wonderful world where a woman can do what she wants to do," Jessie said. "Back in our day, being a teacher was about the top of the heap for a woman. Not that I regret it one bit, and now we have time to travel."

The professor looked up, his blue eyes behind the glasses not focusing on any one person. "Time is a friend to the young."

Shelley welcomed the diversion as she finished the quote. "And a loving enemy for the old."

The professor looked surprised, then smiled at her. "I'm impressed. Not many your age would know that."

Shelley fingered the red linen napkin formed into a rose by her white dinner plate. "English Quotations, 1A. An elective I took my second year in college."

The professor pushed his glasses up farther on his sharp nose. "A quality course, a quality course. Oh, that the young would realize how valuable the English language is in all its forms. But they seem bent on pleasure, a fast solution to life's problems."

"That sounds like your job, doesn't it?" Sloan asked Shelley, not letting go of his last conversation.

Shelley thought of ignoring the man, but knew she couldn't. "How's that?"

"The crook gets the pleasure, then you get him off."

"I never said I did defense law."

Sloan lifted his glass and eyed her over the rim. "No, you didn't. Somehow I just don't see you as a prosecutor."

"I don't see her as an attorney," Brant murmured, then looked past Shelley and frowned. "Ah, another dinner guest," he said.

Shelley turned and looked behind her. When she saw Lucas reaching for the chair next to her, she spoke without thinking. "Oh, it's you."

"Just me," he murmured as he pulled out the empty chair next to her. He glanced around the table at the curious faces. "Hello, everyone. It seems Ms. Kingston and I have cabins next to each other. We met upstairs."

Shelley took a sip of her wine as Lucas settled next to her, then she stared into the pale liquid. She was startled a bit when Brant asked, "So, are you single, Shelley?"

She glanced at him, hating the heat she knew was in her cheeks. "I'm divorced."

"That makes two of us," Brant murmured, then glanced at Lucas. "Everyone else has introduced themselves. How about you?"

"Lucas Jordon," he said as he reached for his water glass. Out of the corner of her eye, Shelley could see his hand close over the crystal. Strong hands, she thought, a scar on the back of his left hand barely evident under the dusting of dark hair on his tanned skin. And no rings. She knew he wasn't married, but she had no idea if there was someone in his life.

"Where are you from, Mr. Jordon?" Jessie asked.

"The city."

"And what do you do?"

He put the water glass on the table but didn't let go of it. He fingered the fine glass with the tips of his fingers, and Shelley forced herself to look away, the idea of being touched by his hand becoming the focal point of her attention suddenly. She reached for her own water glass and took a sip of the cool liquid.

"I work for the city," he said.

"Oh, really, in what capacity?" Lillian asked, not giving up.

Shelley took another sip of water as she wondered what lie Lucas would come up with for these people.

"I work on the pollution situation," he finally said in an even tone.

Shelley nearly choked on her mouthful of water. Quickly, she put down the glass, then pressed her napkin to her mouth as she coughed to catch her breath.

She felt Lucas patting her back, and she tried to move away from the touch as she mumbled, "I...I'm sorry." She coughed, thankful that Lucas had stopped touching her, then she managed to take a breath.

"Did something go down the wrong way?" Lucas asked with apparent innocence.

And when she looked at him, she met his dark gaze and she knew he was daring her to say something about his statement.

"Yes, something did," she managed.

"You have to watch what you swallow," Lucas murmured, and she suddenly realized a disturbing intimacy had passed between them. They were conspirators of sorts, the only two who knew what was going on. And she wanted to break that invisible bond that seemed to be drawing them closer to each other.

Shelley took a quick sip of water again, and thankfully it went down easily this time. She didn't want any sort of bond with this man. All she wanted from him was his protection. The thought was rational and sound. And she believed it until she felt him tap her on her shoulder. The second she felt that contact, she had the sinking feeling that if he touched her again, she would need protection from her own emotions.

Chapter Five

Shelley jerked slightly at the contact from Lucas, and she turned to look at him. His dark eyes met hers, and for a second she felt a soul-deep impact that had little to do with the passing physical contact of moments ago. "Pass the salt, please," he said.

She knew her face had to be bright with color, but she silently reached for the saltshaker and pushed it toward Lucas. She wasn't going to take the chance of handing it to him and touching him again.

"Thanks," he murmured.

The honeymooners stood abruptly, and Rory spoke to no one in particular. "We're going to dance." Then the two of them left the table, their dinners untouched, and headed down to the dance floor.

"Just what do you do about the pollution situation?" Jessie asked Lucas.

"I track down polluters and make sure they are arrested," Lucas said, tapping salt onto the salad the waiter had just put in front of him. "But it's like trying to stop a tank with a squirt gun. You get a case built, take them to court, they get a slap on the hand or maybe a fine, then they're back doing the same thing again. Only this time they're smarter and harder to catch.''

"It sounds like a thankless profession," Brant said.

"It can be," Lucas said. "But I figure that sooner or later it has to start taking effect."

"You're an optimist," Sloan muttered. "The way the law's set up, the guilty get off and the innocent suffer."

Shelley looked at the man, his anger very evident. "Why would you say that?" she asked.

He glared at her. "It's the truth, isn't it? You should know that. Isn't it right that you can't even ask a client if he's guilty? You just have to give the accused a defense. Anyone knows that."

She knew she had never told him exactly what she did, and she wished that she could get Lucas's attention away from the salad he seemed absorbed in. "The law is for everyone, not just the good and the innocent," she said.

Sloan tossed his napkin over his plate. "Bull. That's what makes this system so screwed up."

"Mr. Sloan, I—"

"Goodness, enough of this talk," Lillian said, cutting off Shelley's response.

Shelley looked at the woman, surprised that she spoke up so forcefully. Jessie had seemed to be the spokesperson for the duet. "You're right. Enough of this," she murmured.

"Amen," Brant said.

She glanced at the man, his hazel eyes meeting hers and his smile a flash of perfect white teeth. "We're here to have a good time," he said.

"That's why I'm here," Lucas said as he pushed back his empty salad plate. "And I'm paying enough for the privilege, so let's forget jobs and work and opinions." He picked up his water glass with his right hand and held it out. "Here's to Christmas and a good time."

"Here, here," the professor said, raising his own glass, then the others all followed his lead. Except for Sloan. The man sat staring at his plate, deliberately ignoring the toast.

Shelley felt uncomfortable, and as she put down her glass, she looked away from the table to the dance floor. She immediately spotted the honeymooners dancing to a slow song, holding each other so close the possibility of a gleam of light getting between them was out of the question.

"They should go back to their cabin and do it right," Brant said, and when Shelley looked at him, she could see he had been watching the dancers, too. He put down his napkin, then got up and came around to where Shelley was sitting. When she looked at him, he held out his hand to her. "Dance, pretty lady?"

"Sure, go and dance," Sloan muttered. "This is supposed to be fun." He stared into a drink he held cradled in his hands. "Fun. What a crock."

Brant glared at Sloan, then looked at Shelley. "The music's going to be over if we don't get out there."

Shelley didn't want to dance with Brant. But she didn't want to sit around Sloan any longer, and Lucas wasn't offering her any help at all. "Yes, let's dance," she finally said, and stood. Ignoring Brant's hand, she headed down to the dance floor ahead of him.

Brant was right by her and took her arm, his touch cool on her bare arm. As they stepped out onto the floor, the music changed to "Have Yourself a Merry Little Christmas," and Brant drew her to him. She felt his hand against her back just above the low neckline of the dress, and the touch was vaguely uncomfortable for her. When he spoke, she knew she shouldn't have taken the easy way out. "Those two old ladies are pitiful, aren't they?"

Shelley looked right at him as they began to move to the music. "Why?"

"Retired and on this cruise. This cruise is probably the most exciting thing they've ever done."

"Those two old ladies are Jessie and Lillian Warden, and they seem warm, friendly and intelligent. And I'm sure they've had good lives."

"And what do you think of Sloan?"

She almost missed her step and had to concentrate to keep her feet going in time with the music. "He seems bitter," she responded.

"He seems like a creep to me. The man's got something eating at him, and it looks as if you've brought out the worst in him. Although it's hard for me to understand how you could bring out the worst in anyone." His hand moved lower on her back, dipping to just below her waist, drawing her body more intimately against his.

She tried to be casual and move back, to keep a bit of distance between their bodies. But he wasn't about to let that happen. He did a fancy step, then pulled her against him—hard. "I'm here for fun," he breathed near her ear. "How about you?"

She spotted Lucas at the table, lost in conversation with one of the sisters while they both ate. She felt as if he'd thrown her to the wolves and she was on her own. Not a new situation for her. She bit her lip before she said, "I'm here with my daughter."

Brant drew back just a bit. "Get out of here. You're a mother?"

"Yes."

"I'll be damned," he murmured, then tightened his hold on her again. "That's kind of sexy, though. I've never been with a mommy before."

Shelley put her hand against his shoulder and pushed until she could look at him. "You aren't going to be with one now."

He smiled. "We'll see about that. Maybe I'll let you plead your case, then I'll bring in a verdict. That's kind of sexy, too."

Distaste rose in her throat. "Mr. Weston—"

"Brant, please," he murmured as his hand moved even lower on her back. "And why don't we get out of here?"

Shelley started to tense, but someone touched her shoulder from the back, and as Brant frowned past her, she felt his hold on her ease, letting her turn. Lucas was standing right behind them, and a feeling of being rescued flooded over her. But when she would have pulled free of Brant completely, he wouldn't let her go.

"Dance?" Lucas asked.

"She's dancing with me," Brant said. "Get in line."

"Let's ask the lady," Lucas said without looking away from Shelley.

She glared at Brant and pulled her hand free of his. Without a word to him, she turned to Lucas. "Thank you," she said.

"Later," Brant muttered behind her, then ran a light finger along her bare shoulder as he moved away from her.

Shelley shivered, then Lucas was holding her, his fingers laced with hers, his other hand resting on her waist. As they began to move to the music, he said, "So what's the story with that guy?"

"He's a jerk," she muttered.

"Where does that definitive opinion come from?"

She stared at his chest. "I married one once. I know one when I see one. At least I do now."

His hand shifted on her, its heat on her back, and she moved closer to him. "Older and wiser?"

"Hopefully."

"Where's Emily's father?"

"Off being Peter Pan." She hated the bitterness that could creep into her voice when she spoke about Rob, even after six years of divorce. "He's the kind who never grew up, and didn't want to, but wanted to make very sure he had a woman with him at all times. That woman just didn't happen to be me most of the time."

Lucas moved with surprising ease on the dance floor. "You forgot to say he was a fool, too," he murmured.

She almost missed her step, but Lucas covered it neatly and she murmured, "Thank you."

"What are your instincts about Sloan?"

She resisted the urge to rest her cheek against his chest and kept a bit of distance to look up into his dark eyes. "That man makes me feel very uncomfortable."

"He does that, all right."

"Didn't Bentley check out everyone on the cruise?"

"I'm sure he did. And he must have had everyone at the table checked before he would have had us assigned to it."

"What did he find out about Sloan?"

"I don't know. There wasn't anything in the file he gave me about the table occupants."

"Why not?"

"Not enough time, probably. I'll give him a call later and see what he has."

"Good idea," she breathed, and as they moved to the strains of "The Christmas Song," she began to relax a bit more. At least until she realized she was resting against Lucas, her cheek pressed to his chest and her eyes closed. In an instant she became aware of every place their bodies touched, the heat and strength of him against her, and she began to tense again. But for an entirely different reason this time.

She hadn't enjoyed Brant's touch at all, but she knew if she let herself go just a bit, she could lose herself in Lucas's touch. Strange, she thought. Brant came on to her, and Lucas really couldn't stand her, yet it was all she could do to make herself move back to create some distance between the two of them.

She stared at the fine material of his shirt as she asked, "Do you think whoever wrote the notes and made the calls could be on this ship?"

She could feel him shrug and saw the material of his shirt and jacket move. "I told you before, anything's possible, but it's not likely."

She touched her tongue to her cold lips. "It's hard to believe that someone would hate me so much that they'd follow me here to hurt me."

"Hate makes people do horrendous things." His features tightened. "Horrible things."

She realized that she'd never let her thoughts go to the logical conclusion about the threats. Something had blocked that from her mind until that moment. "Do you *really* think this person wants me dead?"

He looked down at her with shadowed eyes. "I don't know. But it's a possibility."

Her eyes darted past Lucas to the people in the dining room. There were hundreds of strangers, people she'd never met before, yet one of them could want her dead. "Do you think we'll ever know who it is?"

"Maybe not. But even if we catch the person, it might stop you getting hurt, but what good is it going to do beyond that?"

She looked at him. "What do you mean?"

"They'll go to court and maybe their lawyer will find a loophole and they'll walk before you know it." He stared at her. "What does it feel like to know you could be on the wrong end of the legal system, that this creep could be walking the streets again?"

She stopped dancing and drew her hand from his. "I hate to point out the obvious, but if the cops did their job, no one would get back on the streets because of a mistake."

"But what if a mistake's made, what then?"

They faced each other in the middle of the dance floor, and Shelley ignored the furtive glances of the dancers all around them. "Are you talking about a mistake by a cop who's got such a lousy opinion of PDs that he deliberately messes up?"

His expression tightened. "Not on your life."

"That's exactly it. It's my life, mine and Emily's, and you'd better not let your feelings get in the way."

Lucas looked at Shelley standing in front of him, color touching her cheeks and her chin tilted up. Let his feelings get in the way? He could almost laugh at that. Just because she wasn't in his arms, it didn't kill the memory of the feelings he'd had moments ago. Those feelings could have caused a physical display that would have been more than difficult to hide.

Shelley smelled good and felt good, and he wasn't blind to the fact that she was a beautiful woman. "I never let my feelings get in the way," he said, but that didn't stop him from having them.

"Of course not. It's your job," she muttered, and he could see the growing tightness in her expression.

"Exactly." He moved to one side as she walked past him and turned to see her wending her way through the dancers in the direction of the table. He waited until she was sitting down, then he followed her. As much as he'd like to go out onto the deck and get some fresh air not touched by her essence, he knew that he didn't have that luxury.

By the time he got to the table, Shelley was picking at her meal and talking with one of the elderly ladies. He took his seat, careful to maintain a distance between them. She was telling the ladies about Emily, and as Lucas sat back in his seat, he found himself checking his pockets. He'd left the exercise ball in the cabin, and his hand was aching.

He forced himself to spread his sore hand on the tabletop and take a taste of his dessert. As he ate a bit of the rich chocolate cake, he looked up and saw Sloan staring into a highball glass. As he shifted his gaze, he noticed that Brant hadn't come back to the table, and neither had the newlyweds. Then he saw the professor studying him. The man glanced at Lucas's hand. "Did you have an accident?"

Lucas kept from drawing his hand back from where it rested on the white tablecloth. "You might say so." He flexed his fingers. "I was in the wrong place at the wrong time and had a few bones broken and some nerves damaged." He sensed Shelley shifting at his side, but he didn't look away from the professor. "How about you, what brought you on a cruise at Christmas?"

The man sat back. "I don't have any family, and this time of year, there isn't a lot for me to do except attend boring faculty parties at the university and drink too much. Neither appealed to me this year."

Lucas closed his bad hand into a loose fist. That sounded suspiciously like his own holidays for the past few years when he hadn't gone home to spend them with his three brothers and their families. "I can understand why." He looked around the room at the holiday decorations everywhere. "They certainly know how to celebrate around here."

"Christmas," Sloan muttered. "It's a joke."

Lucas looked at the man, at the painfully obvious bitterness in his expression. "Then why are you here?"

Sloan tossed off the last of his drink and motioned to a passing waiter to fill the glass again. "I've got my reasons." He looked around. "Where in the hell is that waiter with my drink?"

Lucas could feel Shelley tensing, and he was shocked that his first instinct was to reach out and put his arm around her. Instead he concentrated on Sloan. "What reasons?"

The man turned and frowned at Lucas. "That's my business." He looked around the table at the others. "I'd bet everyone of you've got secrets, reasons for being here that you wouldn't be about to tell the rest of us." The waiter brought him another drink, and Lucas could tell Sloan was on his way to being very drunk. "To secrets," he muttered as he lifted his re-filled glass.

No one followed suit, but Sloan didn't let that stop him draining the liquid before putting the glass on the table with a cracking thud. He stood, vaguely unsteady on his feet, then without another word walked away from the table. Lucas saw him heading for the piano bar near the entrance to the room.

"Poor man," Lillian murmured.

"My, yes, poor man," Jessie echoed.

"You are both too kind," the professor said.

Shelley moved abruptly to stand. "I think I should get back to my cabin and check on my daughter."

"I'm dying to meet her," Jessie said. "Maybe tomorrow we could explore the ship with the two of you?"

"I'll see what our plans are."

"Wonderful," Lillian said. "I do miss children since we've retired."

Lucas stood. "I think I'll go down, too."

Shelley didn't wait for him to say he'd go with her before she turned and with a murmured good-night to the table, she headed away from him. Lucas followed, watching Shelley ahead of him, and he knew that he was at a distinct disadvantage. From his position, he was inordinately aware of the curve of her hips under the clinging material of her dress, and the expanse of shapely legs.

But when he saw the stiffness in her shoulders and the quickness of her pace, he hurried to catch up to her. As she stepped out of the entrance to the room, he fell in step beside her. Once on the deck, in the coolness of the evening air, he looked at her. The softness of twinkling lights that lined the deck haloed her, touching her with a certain sense of fantasy. He shook his head. He wasn't a fanciful person at all, never had been, but since he'd met this woman, it seemed that he really didn't know himself after all.

Without touching her, he said, "This isn't a race."

She slowed a bit as she approached the elevators, but didn't look at Lucas as she rubbed her arms with her palms. "I've been away from Emily for far too long. It isn't as if we're on this cruise for the fun of it."

"Emily's in good hands."

She stopped at the elevator doors, and as she jabbed the down button, she cast Lucas a slanting glance. Her lavender eyes were shadowed, and the twinkling glow touched the hollows at her cheeks and throat. "Sloan gives me the creeps."

Lucas wouldn't tell her how uneasy the man made him, not until he had time to check the man out, so he simply pointed out the obvious. "He's a drunk, and he's got problems."

"He's also got secrets," she said as she began to tap her foot in impatience when the elevator wasn't forthcoming. "What's taking it so long?" she muttered.

Lucas looked around at the almost deserted deck and said something he didn't know he was going to say until the words were there. "Why don't we take a walk on the deck and give you a chance to calm down a bit before you see Emily?"

She looked at him again. "Is it that obvious?"

"To me it is, but then I know what your secrets are."

She shrugged her slender shoulders. "I hope the others at the table didn't notice."

He motioned to the deck farther down. "There's a phone. Let me make my call to Bentley, then we can take a walk."

She turned and they fell in step, walking through the evening in silence, yet Lucas could sense every breath she took, every thread of tension in her.

When they reached the phone, she moved toward the railing while he put in a shore call to Bentley. After asking for information on the people at their dinner table, he hung up, then crossed to where Shelley was standing.

She turned to him. "Well?"

"He's faxing the backgrounds on everyone to me in a while."

"Good." She started walking again and he fell in step with her. "I'd hate for Emily to see me like this," she said as they approached an open area of the ship near the back. "She knows what's going on, but I've tried to keep it on a low key."

"The child seems to be very mature."

They stopped by the railing, the light breeze stirring the evening air. As Lucas leaned on the railing with his good hand, he stared out at the night, at the glow from the coast off in the distance.

"Emily's very everything," Shelley murmured, and Lucas looked to his right, just far enough to see her hands gripping the rail by his. "She's smart and wise and understands so much. I'm lucky to have her."

Lucas let his gaze travel up her arm, then looked away when he caught a glimpse of her breasts moving with each breath she took. He concentrated on the distant lights. "You've been divorced six years?"

"Yes, but I've been on my own since I got pregnant. It wasn't planned. I was working on my degree, and Rob was getting his footing in his business. I never thought of not having her, but when Rob found out I was pregnant, he didn't want any part of it. He left."

"Just like that?"

"Just like that." He heard her take a low breath. "Don't get me wrong, he's not a bad person, but as I said before, he's a perpetual Peter Pan. Having a child was incomprehensible to him. How could Peter Pan settle down and be a father? That would mean he'd never fly again, and believe me, Rob still wants to fly."

"Does he see Emily at all?"

"Maybe once a year. He's in and out before we really know he's been here at all."

"Emily told me that he travels a lot. Did you tell her that to explain his absence?"

She looked at Lucas, those luxurious lashes shadowing her eyes, but he didn't miss the way her chin tilted just a bit. He was beginning to understand that meant she wasn't happy about something. "I don't lie to my daughter. I tell her the truth. It only hurts more if you let yourself believe in fantasies, then have them shattered. It's better to face the truth and deal with it and get on with your life."

"Is fantasy all bad?"

Her mouth tightened. "It can kill you when it dissolves. I won't let Emily believe in things that can go up in smoke and disappear."

"What things?" he murmured.

"Happily ever after, Prince Charming—"

"And Santa Claus."

"Emily has a right to know exactly what's going on. Pretending that some sweet sprite brings you expensive toys just doesn't wash."

"So, Emily gets to know that toys cost money and that money's hard-earned?"

"You don't agree with that?"

"Maybe. I just think a child should have that magical corner of the world where anything's possible."

"How many children did you say you have?"

"None that I know of, but I *was* a child. I think that counts for something in the experience department."

"That's different," she murmured as she looked off into the distance. "When you're responsible for another life, it changes things completely. All you think about is protecting that person and making sure that they don't get hurt the way you know people can get hurt in this world."

Moonlight touched her profile, and Lucas couldn't help wondering if her job had killed her belief in dreams or if someone like Rob had done that to her. "Didn't you ever think that maybe dreams help cushion the reality of life?"

She shrugged, a fluttery movement of her slender shoulders. "Maybe dreams just make reality all the more painful when it hits you in the face."

This tough PD was dangerously close to becoming a very vulnerable woman to Lucas, and it disturbed him. "I would think with the job you do that you'd nurture dreams instead of denying them."

She turned to look at him. "What?"

"Isn't there enough rough things for a child to deal with in this world without taking away dreams?"

"Dreams are never real, so you can't take them away."

Something in him reacted to this woman on the most basic level, something so strong that he couldn't define it or explain it. An odd mixture of frustration and need, something as strong as hate and as disturbing as pain, yet something that drew him against his will as surely as a moth to a flame. "Dreams feed the soul," he found himself saying.

"So, you let yourself dream?"

He knew the answer to that before the question was completed. Right now he knew that this came precariously close to being a dream. Standing here with a woman who turned everything he did professionally upside down, yet she had him wanting to toss that aside and just see her as a woman. "Oh, I dream," he murmured.

"What about?"

He looked at her for a long moment, catching the moonlight that defined her delicate features, showing the tilt to her chin, the sweep of her long lashes. And without putting the answer in words, he reached out and touched her, his fingers brushing the silky heat of her cheek. Then, before sanity could catch him, he lowered his head and touched her softly parted lips with his.

Chapter Six

There was no justification for it, no basis in rational thinking, but at that moment, all Lucas wanted was to know the taste of Shelley, to pull her into a world of dreams and soft wonder. A world where fantasies endured and the reason for his presence on this ship and in her life were pushed away. A world where it didn't matter that she fought everything he stood for. It was just a man and a woman. The dream held more potency than anything he'd ever dreamed of in his life.

Shelley felt her breath catch in her chest when Lucas touched her. She knew she should move, that she should break the contact, but the feeling of his fingers on her face riveted her to the spot. Nothing made sense about this, but when his lips found hers, she knew something totally remarkable. She wanted him to kiss her.

Despite what he thought of her and what she knew made sense, she had wanted him to touch her like this since she'd faced him toe-to-toe in the courtroom. And the awareness when they'd been dancing had just been a hint of this. Even though his touch was vaguely tentative now, almost as if the action surprised him as much as it did her, it rocked her.

She couldn't move. She couldn't raise her hands and circle his neck, or bring his body against hers. Instead there were the tantalizingly inadequate contacts where her breasts brushed his chest and his hands captured her face. His tongue teased her with a feathery suggestion of invasion, grazing her lips, then her teeth.

Dreams? God, the dreams this man could bring with his touch were staggering. Dreams of holding on to him, feeling his body against hers, feeling, touching, knowing. As his hands moved on her, catching her closer to him, Shelley knew just how potent the possibility of dreaming that way could be.

Her whole body responded in a way it never had before. It slipped into a world that was filled with sensations and needs. Heady, needful things. Dreams that she hadn't let herself even acknowledge for years. As Lucas trailed his mouth to a sensitive hollow on the side of her throat, she came full circle. Dreams that could hurt and destroy. A coldness invaded Shelley, and she trembled.

Lucas drew back, framing her face with his hands and studying her with shadowed eyes. She could feel the need in him, the hard arousal that let her know he was close to letting go of logic and reality, as close as she was. And that couldn't happen. She closed her eyes for a moment, then turned away from his touch, and the instant the contact was gone, she felt an isolation that physically hurt.

"Don't," she breathed unsteadily, "don't."

He didn't touch her again, and a part of her grieved for that, while another part felt distinctly thankful.

"Why?" he asked in a low, hoarse voice.

She couldn't look at him, and the lights of the coastal cities were blurring in front of her. "This... this whole thing, it doesn't change anything."

"Excuse me? What was that?"

She closed her eyes, hating the burning behind her lids. "Just because this happened, it doesn't change reality."

"What's your version of reality, Shelley?"

Her hands clenched on the slick railing. "You're here because it's your job, not because of a burning need to protect a PD who's getting death threats."

"A burning need?" he whispered.

She remembered the feel of him against her, and swallowed hard. "You know what I mean." When he didn't say a thing, she finally turned, her nerves stretched to the breaking point. He was studying her, his eyes shadowed, but she could feel the intensity in the man. "Don't you?"

"Absolutely," he murmured.

"Good. Then let's forget this happened."

"Absolutely."

"It's over and done."

"Absolutely."

Her nerves were raw. "And stop that!"

"Stop what?"

"Saying that."

He studied her for a long moment, not moving, not talking, and just when she thought she was going to scream, he tensed. She saw his hand move, and she knew she couldn't deal with him touching her again. It was hard enough to collect herself after the kiss. But in the next instant, his hand was on her arm, not pulling her to him, but jerking her to one side away from the railing.

She twisted away, freeing herself of his hold, then turned and in a single moment that seemed to last for an eternity, she saw Lucas thrust his fist out as James Sloan lunged right at him. Lucas struck Sloan in the middle of his chest, and as curses mingled in the air, both men staggered backward.

Sloan flailed his arms, but hit the deck flat on his back, and his head bounced on the wood. Lucas lurched, then righted himself and seemed to dive at Sloan. But the next thing Shelley knew, Lucas was crouched by the prone man, grabbing at the front of his jacket with his right hand. Shelley hurried to where the two men were and looked at Sloan. The man's eyes were open but glazed, and the smell of alcohol was strong in the air. Lucas jerked the man upward, and Sloan's head lolled back.

"Hey, hey," Sloan mumbled, his hands futilely pushing at Lucas's grip on him. "You...you...shop...stop..."

Lucas exhaled, then did as Sloan asked, letting him drop to the deck. Then he stood, and Shelley stepped back to keep from making contact with him.

"What happened?"

Lucas gripped his left arm with his right hand and started rubbing at it through his jacket. "The bastard. He's sloshed." He cast Shelley a look. "I saw him coming up behind you. I thought—" He clenched his fist again and addressed Sloan. "Get up."

Sloan stared at Lucas. "You hit me."

"Don't I wish," Lucas muttered. "Get up and get out of here." He offered Sloan a hand.

Sloan muttered a curse and rolled to one side, grabbing at the railing for support. Awkwardly he got to his feet, then grabbed the top rail to stay upright. "I need a drink," the man mumbled as he ran a hand over his face.

"What were you doing?"

Sloan looked at Lucas. "I was just goin' to talk to the lady," he said, his words slurred.

"Me?" Shelley asked.

Sloan looked at her. "Yeah. Thought you might like to go for a drink." He waved a hand to the side and struck his knuckles on the railing. But he acted as if nothing had happened. "Forget it. It's late. I...I need to..."

"Sleep it off," Lucas said.

"Sure. Sleep." Sloan staggered to the right, then keeping his hold on the rail, he headed toward the front of the ship.

Shelley rubbed at her arms with her hands. "I never even heard him coming."

"I saw him, but I didn't know it was Sloan until he was on the ground."

"What a miserable man." She turned to see Lucas grimacing as his fingers kneaded his shoulder, his eyes staring down the deck after Sloan.

"He's a jerk, and I probably overreacted." He shook his head and turned toward the railing. "Damn, I'm out of practice."

"What did you think he was going to do?"

His hand on his shoulder stilled as Lucas looked at Shelley. "I don't know. Dump you over the rail or something, I guess."

She glanced down at the dark waters around the ship, and the almost iridescent foam that was being left in its wake. It looked mysterious and frightening. She knew Lucas was exaggerating, but she shivered anyway. "James Sloan is an ugly man."

"More than that."

As she looked at Lucas, she could feel the space around them beginning to shrink again. She couldn't handle the way the world narrowed when she was this close to the man. "What is he, then?"

"I don't know. Maybe he just wants us to think he's a drunk out of control."

"I don't understand."

"People show you what they want you to see, sometimes for valid reasons and sometimes for ulterior motives."

Despite the warmth in the air, she could feel a chill deep inside. "I thought at the table he might... I mean, he was so pointed in his comments. I didn't know if he meant it, or if he was just baiting me."

Lucas looked up and down the deck, then said, "Let's go back down to the cabins. It's too open out here."

As he turned to head for the elevators, she fell in step beside him. "Bentley had Sloan checked, you said he did, and if Sloan was a threat in any way, Bentley would have made sure he wasn't anywhere near where we were, wouldn't he?"

He didn't look at her as they approached the elevators. "If the check was complete."

"What check? What does he do exactly?"

"They go through computers, records of any sort, you know, DMV, service records, criminal checks, employers. With computers it's getting easier and easier for Big Brother to know everything about you. But it still takes time."

"And Bentley did that with everyone on board?"

"He's working on it. And he's checking everyone you're likely to come close to."

"That sounds pretty complete," she said as they stopped by the elevators.

Lucas pushed the down button. "Yeah, it should be. But it's still human beings working the computers. And they're fallible."

"You aren't making me feel very secure."

He slanted her a look as a soft chime sounded and the elevator doors slid open. "Things slip by people, or they read a situation wrong. Look at what I just did to a slobbering drunk."

He stepped into the empty car and turned. Shelley met his gaze for just a minute, but it was long enough for her to remember every detail of the kiss earlier. Quickly, she looked away and stepped into the car, keeping as much distance between herself and Lucas as she could.

As the doors slid shut, Shelley turned and found her reflection bouncing back at her off the polished surface of the doors, with Lucas near her side. She could see him grimace and flex his fingers. "Did you hurt yourself?"

His hand stilled as his dark eyes met hers in the metal reflection. "Not really, but I shouldn't have tried to be his tackling dummy."

"Maybe you shouldn't have come back to work so soon."

The car slid silently down. "This isn't exactly like working a shift. I know some guys who'd kill for it."

"Then how did you get so lucky?"

"No family close by, no plans, no way I could go back on regular duty. It all adds up to this."

"Baby-sitting?"

The elevator stopped and Lucas moved, but he didn't get out. He stood in the doorway and seemed impervious to the door bouncing softly off his back as it tried to close over and over again. He looked at her with dark eyes, eyes that made her feel as if he could look into her soul and see the turmoil there every time she looked at him. "I'm your bodyguard. And on deck...that should have never happened. I'm sorry."

She didn't have to ask what he was talking about, and she couldn't think of a thing to say to him right then about the kiss. Instead, she stepped past him and into the corridor. She made very sure she didn't touch him at all.

She heard him coming behind her, but she didn't stop until she got to the door of her cabin. As she reached for the door latch, Lucas was right there, and his hand caught hers. The contact produced a sudden and intense awareness in her that made her gasp, and she jerked her hand back. She turned toward him, only to find him mere inches from her, way too close for comfort.

"I just apologized to you, Ms. Kingston."

"I know you did."

"You should know that I don't do that very often."

She made herself meet his gaze. "The cop who's always right, who never backs down or makes mistakes?"

"I'm not always right. Not even close." For a split second he glanced at her lips, and she had the idea that he was going to kiss her again. But he didn't, and for some crazy reason, she felt an annoying tinge of regret. "I was way out of line on deck earlier."

"What do you want me to say?" she breathed.

The cabin door opened suddenly, and Shelley turned to see Martha there. The woman stared at the two of them as she let out a long, hissing breath. "Oh, it's you two. I heard something out here and I . . ."

"How's everything?" Lucas asked Martha.

"Just fine. The little one's asleep. There was a call for you," she said to Shelley. "Someone from Bentley's office called and said that a man from your office needs you to contact him as soon as you can. The name's on the notepad by the phone."

"Thanks," Shelley said as she went into the room past Martha without looking at Lucas again. She glanced at Emily curled up in her bed, the covers over her and her hands folded under her cheek. Then she reached for the notepad on the table that separated the beds and saw the name Ryan Sullivan scrawled on it.

She turned and saw Lucas had come into the cabin and closed the door.

"Martha, how long ago did they call?"

Martha glanced at the wall clock. "Half an hour at the most."

Lucas strode across the room to the connecting door, then cast Shelley a dark look. "I'll let you make your call and see you in the morning. If you need anything or if anything out of the ordinary happens, get me."

"I will," she murmured.

He nodded to Martha, then went into his cabin, closing the door behind him. Shelley looked at Martha. "I don't know how to thank you for all your help."

"I enjoyed it." She looked down at Emily and smiled. "Children are so trusting and innocent. It's a shame that doesn't last very long. They're gone before you know it."

"I know. Emily's growing up too quickly." She looked at the woman. "Do you have children?"

Martha shook her head, the smile faltering a bit. "No, I never had the chance, but I love them." She looked at Shelley. "You know, I meant to give you my references before, but I totally forgot. They're in my cabin."

"I'd like that. Thank you."

Martha looked at Shelley. "You can't be too careful where children are concerned, can you?"

"No, you can't."

"And children do have such a lovely time while it lasts, don't they? Especially at Christmas. I told Emily I'd take her up to the Santa Claus party tomorrow afternoon."

"I don't know . . ."

"And they'll put a Christmas tree in your room if you'd like."

"No, thanks. We aren't much on Christmas."

"The little lady said that she doesn't believe in Santa Claus."

"No, she doesn't." Before Martha could get into a discussion about it, Shelley said, "I really need to make this call."

"Just call when you need me tomorrow. I'm up early, so don't hesitate. I left my cabin number on the pad with your message."

"Thanks so much," Shelley said as she crossed to the door to get it for the woman.

After Martha left, Shelley locked the door, then crossed to her bed and sank down on the edge. She put through the call to Ryan, and when he answered after three rings, she could hear his relief in his voice.

"Thank goodness it's you."

"What's going on?"

"It's the Moran case. The DA offered a plea bargain on it to burglary two, with two to four years and credit for time served."

Shelley hated to see that happen. Charlie Moran was a basically good kid in a bad life, and she hated to see him saddled with a felony. "Tell the DA that Charlie Moran gets it cut down to a misdemeanor, credit for time served and a rehab program through the courts. We'll go for that."

"And if he won't go for it?"

"Tell him we'll see him in court and see just how strong his evidence is. I don't think it'll stick if he pushes for a felony on it."

"I'll contact him in the morning and tell him."

"Thanks, Ryan."

"So, how's the fugitive doing?"

She grimaced at his choice of words. "Just fine."

"Do they have you holed up in a mountain cabin where the only neighbors are twenty miles through foot-deep snow and mountain lions roam around outside all night with the wolves?"

"What?"

"Isn't that what they do? They set you up in some remote place on the top of a mountain where only a psycho mountain goat can get to you?"

"Sure, of course," she said, then asked, "has anything happened there?"

"You've only been gone for eight hours."

It felt like forever to her, another world, another life. "I guess so. I'll call you back tomorrow at the office to find out what the DA's office is going to do for Moran."

"Good. Shelley, take care of yourself and Emily."

"Sure."

"And have a very merry Christmas, wherever you are."

"Thanks, you, too," she said, then hung up.

As she moved around the quiet cabin getting out of her clothes and into a nightshirt, she tried to focus on the Moran case, hoping against hope that the DA wouldn't push it onto the court calendar. But as she brushed her hair, she was inordinately aware of every sound from Lucas's cabin. A thud, then a dull thump and silence. She put down the brush, then flipped off the overhead lights and crossed to the bed.

She got into bed and slid down into the cool linen, and with the rhythmic motion of the ship acting like a sedative, Shelley drifted to sleep. The last thing she thought of was the moment on the deck with Lucas, his lips on hers.

SHE CAME TO HIM in a dream.

Lucas knew he was sleeping, that he was alone in the huge bed in the cabin, yet Shelley was with him. If he inhaled, he would be filled with her essence, the soft, flowery scent that clung to her. If he reached out, he would touch her, feel the satiny heat of her skin under his hands and be able to trace the sweep of her jaw with his fingers.

He could feel his body begin to tighten, and in the dream, he knew anything was possible. The world could shift in dreams. Reality could be blocked, blotting out things in his mind and letting Shelley come to him through the mists of dreams.

He could go to her without hesitation, reaching out and pulling her to him. Reality could be gone for a heartbeat or an eternity. And he let it happen. She was there, her hands out to him. Then she was with him, holding him, and he felt as if he could barely take in his next breath.

He buried his face in the tumble of her curls, then his lips found her temple, her eyes, her lips, and he tasted her, the heat and sweetness echoing from reality into the dream. Her taste filled him, and he was flooded with need. He was over her, his body covering her, her breasts pressed to his chest, her heart echoing its beat against his, and he felt as if he could absorb her into himself, that she could become one with him.

And in that instant, he knew that even when he woke, a need for her would be with him. He felt his heart lurch, then she was gone. He reached out to emptiness, to a void that he hated, and in that instant, he was wrenched into wakefulness.

He opened his eyes to the shadows of his cabin, his hands pressed to the bed at his sides, his shoulder in agony and his body tight and aching with a need that hadn't even come close to being met. He muttered a low oath and sat up, throwing his legs over the side of the bed, then he got to his feet and padded across the carpet to the bathroom. He ignored the painkillers on the vanity and reached for a bottle of aspirin. Quickly he took two white pills, washed them down with bottled water on a tray by the sink, then turned to avoid his own image in the mirror.

He went into the quietness of the cabin and glanced at the digital clock by the bed. Six o'clock. Morning. And he felt as if he hadn't slept at all. He raked his fingers through his hair, then crossed to the closet and took out white cotton slacks and a pale blue T-shirt. As he dressed, then slipped on his shoes, he spotted a large envelope under his cabin door. He picked it up, then took out a fax with the information Bentley had promised.

As he scanned the list of people, he heard something in the next cabin. He stopped, waited, then heard it again, a strange blipping electronic sound. He tossed the envelope on the dresser and crossed to the connecting door. He heard the sound again, followed by a giggle that sounded like Emily, then rapped on the wood.

The door opened a moment later, but instead of Shelley standing in front of him, he saw Martha in a garish pink shift with her damp hair tightly combed against her head. "Mr. Jordon, good morning," she said with a smile.

He glanced past her but couldn't see Shelley. Emily was sitting on the floor in front of the television, and a video game was flashing on the screen. "You're all up early, aren't you?"

"I'm an early riser, and so's Emily. We got a video game from the purser and we're going to the Santa Claus party later on."

"Where's Shelley?"

Emily looked at him over her shoulder, the soft blue of her sunsuit making her eyes even more lavender. "My mommy's gone."

He moved past Martha in an instant to go to stand over the child. "What did you say?"

Emily shrugged and turned back to the game. "She got up early and Martha came to visit, so Mommy left for a while. She said she'd be back for breakfast."

Lucas turned to Martha. "Where did she go?"

Martha shrugged and crossed to sit on the nearest bed. "She didn't say. I didn't like it, her going off on her own and all, not with the situation as it is, but she insisted. She said she'd be fine and she'd be back by eight."

"She knows she's not supposed to go anywhere on her own. You shouldn't have let her go."

"I wasn't about to tackle her, Mr. Jordon. She's not a prisoner."

Lucas controlled an urge to shake the woman and asked, "Don't you have *any* idea where she could be?"

"She was in her bathing suit," Martha finally said.

"Thanks," Lucas muttered, wondering if it would have killed her to say that any earlier. He headed into his cabin, got his gun and pushed it into his waistband under his shirt, then looked into the other cabin. "I'll be back soon. Stay with Emily," he said.

"I planned to," Martha said grimly.

"And if Shelley comes back before I do, tell her she's to stay right here and wait for me."

"I sure will," she said as he turned and left.

By the time Lucas got to the deck where the pools were, he was feeling short of breath and his heart was racing. Christmas music was already being piped in, and crew members were setting up the portable bars and decorating them with holly and red ribbons. Christmas trees were everywhere, small, large, green, blue, but it had never felt less like Christmas to Lucas than now.

His shoulder hurt like hell despite the aspirin he'd taken, and he was torn between being angry with Shelley for leaving without him and being afraid that something might have happened to her.

When he spotted the pool area and headed toward it at a jog, he saw a scattering of people near the main area. Then off to one side he heard children laughing and splashing in a smaller pool. He almost turned to go to the larger pool, but he stopped when he spotted Shelley on the side of the small pool with a group of small children.

Relief almost made him dizzy, then the sight of her in a sleek maillot brought back memories of the dream, and his body tightened. Long, slender legs, the swelling of her hips, skin that looked creamy. He swallowed hard and would have started for her, depending on his anger to get him through a face-to-face confrontation.

But he stopped when a man on the far side of the pool called out, "Everyone in the pool."

Shelley eased down the edge of the pool, then slipped into water that was shoulder high for the children, but waist high for her. Then Lucas knew what was going on, and it was all he could do to keep a grip on the anger that had driven him this far.

Shelley wasn't in any danger at all, at least not from some stalker. He sank down in one of the deck chairs near the pool and stared at her. She was taking a damned swimming lesson, and he was overreacting. His emotions were spinning out of control.

Chapter Seven

"Now, hold your noses and get wet," the instructor called out.

The kids varied from being afraid to do it, to squealing and diving in, but Shelley stood there all but frozen. Water terrified her. If she was on it, she was fine. If she drank it or bathed in it, she was all right. But being surrounded by it made her feel like she was suffocating. When she'd spotted the ad for swimming lessons, she'd decided it was time to take them, but she hadn't realized all the others in the class would be children.

She looked at the kids, most of them getting into the spirit of dunking and bobbing out of the water, then the instructor called out, "Shelley, come on, it's your turn."

She could feel her heart racing, but she knew that she didn't have a choice. She held her nose, closed her eyes, prayed that she wouldn't embarrass herself, then forced herself to go down into the warm water. But the moment she was completely under, she lost all orientation, and in a panic she let go of her nose and gasped.

As she sucked in water, she lost her footing and felt herself going backward into the weightlessness. Flailing her arms as water invaded her nose, mouth and eyes, she grabbed for anything to stabilize herself. She felt something rough under her hand and grabbed it. Pulling hard, she surged upward and was out of the water, sputtering and choking, holding on to the side so tightly the cement was pressing into her skin.

The instructor was there, asking if she was okay, but as she coughed and gasped for air and swiped at her face with her free hand, she was sure she was hallucinating.

Either she was imagining Lucas sitting in a deck chair about ten feet from her, staring at her, a witness to her embarrassment, or he was really there. When she met his gaze and felt the impact of the anger smoldering there, she knew he was more than real. She mumbled something to the instructor about being all right, but she could feel heat flooding her face.

She wished she had the nerve to slip under the water and disappear. But if she tried that, she'd just end up coughing and looking like a soaked rat again. There he was in casual clothes with his hair slicked back and the clear morning light shining on his chiseled features while he stared at her.

She turned away from him and stared blindly at the children all around her. This had been a mistake from the word go, and she just wanted to get out and leave. But she couldn't do that as long as Lucas was there watching. She let go of her death grip on the coping and tried to listen to what the instructor was saying.

"Now that we're all wet, we're going to learn to fly in the water. It's called floating." He spread his arms out at his sides. "Just put your arms out and ease backward and let yourself go."

As Shelley watched the man lay back and start to float on the water, she could feel her stomach tense at the idea of following his lead. She tried to build up her courage, tried to make herself relax enough to try it, but nothing worked. Then the instructor called, "Everyone out and to the side of the pool."

Shelley was more than glad to get out, and as she managed to lever herself up and out, she made a point of not looking anywhere near where Lucas had been sitting. When she got out, she barely had time to stand on the decking before Lucas was by her, his hand closing over her upper arm. Then he called out to the instructor, "We have to leave. It's an emergency."

Shelley glared at Lucas and tried to free herself, but she couldn't get away from his hold. And short of causing a scene right there, she knew she had little choice but to go with him. "What are you doing?" she demanded in a whisper.

He stared at her, and she'd never felt more exposed in her life than under the scrutiny of those dark eyes at that moment. "Saving your butt," he muttered and looked around. "Get your things. We have to go."

She quickly reached for her towel, cover-up and sandals on the chair by her, but didn't have time to do more than clutch them to her before Lucas jerked her toward him and they were heading across the deck.

She had to skip to keep up with his determined stride, and he didn't stop until they were in an alcove by vending machines near stairs that led down to the lower decks. When she pulled to get free, he let her go so easily that she almost stumbled against the side wall. As she righted herself, she turned to him and found his expression filled with palpable anger. "I am not that damn red ball of yours, so don't ever do that to me again," she said.

"Wrong hand," he muttered.

She dropped the things in her arms to the floor and grabbed the cover-up. As she pushed her arms into the terry-cloth robe, she demanded, "How could you do that in front of everyone?"

He glared at her. "I thought you were intelligent, that I could count on you to understand what I say to you."

She could feel heat in her cheeks as she did up the tie at her waist. "Of course I understand. Don't patronize me."

"Then why in the hell did you take off like that?"

She stooped to pick up her sandals and towel, then looked at Lucas. "I wanted to—to..." She faltered. "I didn't think about—"

"Wonderful," he muttered. "You didn't think. It's just your life, lady."

"I know," she said, things brought into painful focus with his words. "It is my life. But I didn't choose this turn of events."

"Of course you didn't. Neither did I. But we're here, so get used to it." He exhaled as if to get his control, then he said, "And get used to the rules. Rule number one is you don't go *anywhere* without telling me. Rule two is—"

"All right, all right," she muttered as cool water from her hair found its way under her collar and down her back. "You've made your point."

He startled her by thrusting his right hand out, but not to touch her. He hit the wall behind her somewhere near her left shoulder, then rocked toward her, coming so close that she could see gold shot in the irises of his eyes. "I don't think I have."

She forced herself to stay very still so she wouldn't chance making anymore contact with Lucas. "Trust me, you have."

"Let's hope so," he murmured, then drew back. "From now on, if you're going to take swimming lessons, I'm tagging along. I don't care where you go or what you do, I'll be there."

"I'd hate to think what you'd do if you really thought the psycho was on the ship," she muttered.

He stared at her. Hard. Then murmured, "I'd chain you to the bed for the rest of the cruise."

Heat flared in her cheeks. "Oh, would you?"

"It would be my distinct pleasure," he said, then moved back a bit. "Now, *we'll* go down to the cabins," he said and would have reached to take her arm again, but she pulled away just before he could make the contact. When he drew back, she cast him a nervous glance, shielding herself from the full impact of his dark gaze by lowering her lashes. "Let's go," she muttered, then turned from him and went into the stairwell.

As she started down, her bare feet made no sound on the steps, but his shoes made a ringing echo with each impact, not letting her forget how close he was.

Hugging her sandals and towel to her, she hurried down, anxious to get to her cabin and away from the man.

Lucas knew this was all out of control, but when he was around Shelley, he didn't seem quite capable of thinking in a rational, nonemotional pattern. And having the dream he'd had didn't help, either. The woman seemed to be planted in his mind, a seed that was growing and growing into something that he was at a loss to remove.

When they got to their deck and headed out of the stairwell into the corridor, he kept his distance behind her. He watched her ahead of him, her hair, darkened by the water, clinging to her head and shoulders. He didn't allow himself to look lower. There was no reason to remind himself about her body. God knew he had enough trouble keeping his focus just being close to her.

He raked his fingers through his hair and wondered where the angry feelings he'd had about her had fled to since he'd met her. She was what she was. So was he. And if he'd made a list of what he'd look for in a woman—*if* he was looking for a woman—she would have qualified in sexiness and looks, but not in any other way. Besides, she had a child. That would have been a major block for Lucas if there had been any way a relationship could have developed.

When they reached her cabin, he opened the door for her, saw Martha and Emily inside, then motioned her to go in. When he followed her inside, he had the distinct impression she wished she could slam the door in his face. She didn't do or say anything, but she cast him a look from those lavender eyes that said, *Get lost*.

He ignored it as he closed the door behind him and looked at Martha and Emily huddled on one of the beds, bent over a huge book. They both looked up, and Emily frowned at her mother. "You're all wet. How come? You can't swim."

Shelley tossed her things on the empty bed. "I went to take a swimming lesson so I could go swimming with you."

Emily's face lit up. "Oh, good. We can go together and you won't get all sick swallowing the water!"

"I'm afraid I didn't learn very much. For now, you're going to have to show me how you do it, but someday we'll swim together."

Martha put down the book, then slid off the bed. "If you're going to be here for a while, I have a few things I need to take care of." She looked at her wristwatch. "How about I come back about eleven and take Emily to the big party?"

Shelley had a hard time letting Emily out of her sight, even if Martha had been picked by Bentley. "I don't know. I thought we could have lunch and—"

"But, Mommy, the party's going to be wonderful. Please can I go?"

She hated her need to hold onto Emily and never let her go. "I don't know."

"I won't let her out of my sight," Martha said, then looked at Lucas. "What do you think?"

Lucas shrugged. "If you'll stay right with her and let us know if you go anywhere else, I think it would be all right."

Martha looked at Shelley. "Is that okay with you?"

She felt as if she'd been outnumbered completely, and reluctantly agreed. "I guess so."

"I'll see you at eleven." Martha ruffled Emily's hair, then headed to the door. As she approached Lucas, she spoke in a low voice that didn't carry to Shelley and Emily by the bed. "Is everything all right?"

"What makes you ask that?"

"You look ready to spit nails," she said.

He hoped he wasn't that easy to read. "Everything is just fine."

She nodded and patted him on the chest. "If you say so." Then she called over her shoulder, "See you," and left, closing the door behind her.

Lucas stared at the door, then at Shelley. She was on the bed with Emily in her lap and the huge book open in front of them. "And it says here that Santa Claus was first called Saint Nicholas," Emily was saying with real animation. "And that he was like a real man, and he was kind and nice to kids, and he did good things for people." Emily twisted to look at her mother. "Is that true?"

"That's history. It's true," Shelley said.

Emily hesitated, then said, "Do you suppose that maybe it could be like that now?"

"Like what?"

"That there's people like that who do good things and give kids gifts at Christmas and things like that?"

"Of course, there is." She tapped her daughter's nose. "They're called mommies and daddies."

Emily looked at the book, then at Shelley. "You don't think that maybe—"

"Sweetheart," Shelley said, closing the book. "Why don't you go and get dressed, then we'll go up for breakfast?"

"But, Mommy, I—"

"Emily, we need to get up to breakfast before everyone eats all the food."

Emily stood and although her lip was out just a bit, she turned and headed for the bathroom. When the door shut, Shelley looked at Lucas. "It is all right to go to breakfast, isn't it?"

He shrugged, not about to admit that that hadn't been his thought right then. He'd been fascinated by Shelley dealing with the child. "Children want to believe in magic, don't they?" he asked.

She stood and grabbed the towel off the bed and began to towel her hair. The blond strands were partially dry, showing a surprising hint of curl. "Are we going to go through this again?"

"No, we aren't," he said quickly and started across the room to his cabin. "Breakfast. Half an hour. We'll go up together."

"Is that a good idea?" she asked.

He turned to look at her, the towel wrapped around her hair turban style, exposing the gentle lines of her face and throat. "Why wouldn't it be?"

"I didn't think that you thought we should be seen together too much."

He shrugged. "Since everyone knows we have cabins next to each other, and after we danced together last night, I'm sure that Lillian and Jessie won't think a thing about it."

"Whatever you say," she said.

"Exactly." He opened the door to his cabin, but stopped and turned. "Oh, James Sloan."

"What about him?"

"I got Bentley's fax this morning just before I found you. The man's wife was killed in a car accident a year ago, and he's been drinking himself to death ever since."

He saw the instant sympathy in Shelley for the man, and he found himself adding in a voice that was cooler than he intended, "The driver of the other car had had his license suspended for another accident earlier in the year. But his attorney got him off with probation. He shouldn't have been driving the night he killed Sloan's wife."

Shelley just looked at Lucas. There was no reason for either of them to say anything else. He turned and slipped into his cabin and swung the door shut after him. He crossed to the bed and picked up the ball he'd left sitting in a bowl on the side table, and despite the pain that throbbed in his arm and hand, he gripped it hard as he stared at the closed door.

"LUCAS?" Emily tugged at the sleeve of the white T-shirt Lucas was wearing with jeans. He was sitting beside the child at the table in the dining area, and watched Shelley at the breakfast buffet with Lillian and Jessie, discussing something about the steaming dishes of eggs and bacon. She'd pulled her hair back in a low ponytail and wore a loose white dress with a low waist and thin shoulder straps that set off the faint tan of her skin.

"Lucas?" Emily said again, tugging on his arm.

"What is it?" he asked without looking away from Shelley.

"What does impudent mean?"

He turned and looked at her, her hair tightly braided back from her face and her large eyes narrowed in a frown. The pink of her sundress added color to her cheeks, and for a second Lucas had the crazy idea that this was probably how Shelley must have looked at Emily's age.

"Well, what does impudent mean?" she persisted.

Lucas had been so involved in keeping an eye on Shelley that he hadn't been paying attention to the goings-on at the table. He glanced at Sloan and the professor, who sat across from them, then at Emily. "Impudent means that you're being rude and you've got an attitude."

Emily flashed a glaring look at James Sloan who, despite the crisp freshness of a white shirt and his hair combed straight back from his face, looked as if he'd had a rough night. And from the looks of the half-empty Bloody Mary in his hand, his day wasn't much better.

"I am not impudent, Mr. Sloan," Emily said.

Sloan shook his head, then grimaced and drained his glass. "You sure are, big time, kid." He glared at Lucas. "And you keep crummy company."

Emily gave him a look that should have cut him to the bone. "I keep *real* good company," she said with conviction. "And I don't have an attitude, either." When Sloan banged down his empty glass, Emily sidled closer to Lucas and whispered, "What's an attitude, Lucas?"

He would have laughed if she hadn't been so sincere. "Do you know what it means when someone acts as if they know everything and that they're great and look down at you for not knowing what they know?" He kept his voice low. "Or when they act hot?"

She nodded. "Yeah."

"That's having an attitude."

She turned to glare at Sloan. "*You* have an attitude, Mr. Sloan."

The man was in the process of getting to his feet, and with a dismissive wave of his hand and a muttered, "Forget it," he turned and started to make his way across the room to the exit.

"What a jerk," Emily muttered.

"Just what did he say to you?" Lucas asked.

She sat back, her arms crossed over her chest. "He asked me what Santa Claus was bringing me for Christmas, and I told him that my mommy's getting me some clothes and stuff, sensible things, and that Santa doesn't get anyone anything, that Santa Claus was a nice, kind man a long time ago, but he isn't now."

Lucas tried to keep a straight face. "And what did he say about that?"

"He said that wasn't so, and I told him that it was, too, and that it was stupid to believe it. Stanley Weed was just like Mr. Sloan, and he wanted to fight me."

"Mr. Sloan?"

"No, Stanley Weed, but Mr. Sloan just said that I was awful and I said I wasn't, and he said I was impudent."

Lucas had had very little to do with children during his life, both by circumstance and by choice, even his nieces and nephews. He never felt comfortable around them, nor was he capable of seeing them as little human beings. But he knew that a child of seven shouldn't be this serious about being able to refute someone, even Sloan, who talked about Santa. "I guess he thought you were saying he was stupid."

She cocked her head to one side and studied Lucas. "What do you think?" she asked. "Isn't it stupid for someone as old as he is to be saying things like that?"

He hedged. "Sloan's stupid, I guess."

"And am I impudent?" she asked.

"I'd say you're just being honest."

She looked at him intently. "But am I impudent?" she persisted.

"No, you aren't," he said. "But you've got beautiful eyes."

Emily actually blushed at that and giggled. "I don't, either, do I?"

"Well, what's so funny?" Shelley asked as she took her place on the other side of Emily.

Lucas glanced at her, a bit annoyed that just seeing her could make his body tighten. But he wasn't surprised. Her incredible lavender gaze was on her child. "Lucas said that I'm not impudent."

"He what?"

"Mr. Sloan said that I'm impudent, but Lucas says that I'm honest and I've got pretty eyes. He says that means I'm not impudent and I don't have an attitude."

Shelley looked at Lucas over Emily's head, the shade of her eyes deep and true. "What's this all about?"

He shrugged. "Sloan was being obnoxious."

Shelley glanced at Sloan's empty seat. "Where did he go?"

"He left," Emily said. "You know, I think he's like that man who came to see us a while ago, the one who smelled funny."

"Yes, you're right, he does drink like Mr. Marley did."

"I could tell," Emily said.

"You're very perceptive," Shelley said with a smile for Emily.

The child turned to Lucas. "That means that I understand things. Mommy told me that before."

Lucas watched Shelley. "I bet she did."

"That man is dreadful," Jessie said from across the table by Sloan's empty chair. Both Jessie and Lillian had been taken with Emily from the moment Shelley, Lucas and Emily had come in for the breakfast buffet, and now the lady smiled at Emily. "I heard what you've been saying, and I think you should just ignore him, sweetheart. I've got a good mind to see if we can get him taken off this table."

"Oh, don't do that," Shelley said. "The man's had a lot of problems."

"What sort of problems?" the professor asked.

"He lost his wife a while ago."

"Now, how would you know that?" Lillian asked.

Shelley looked taken aback for a moment, then shrugged. "Why, he mentioned it last night when I ran into him on deck. He was very drunk, and he was talking a bit."

"That's odd, indeed," Jessie murmured. "He told us he didn't have any family."

"Maybe his wife was all the family he had."

"You're right, dear," Lillian said. "I guess what he said about secrets is more than painfully true for him." She looked right at Shelley, the gentle politeness that usually touched her face gone, replaced by a tightness at her mouth and eyes. "Secrets can do great damage to one's self and to others."

"Did I hear someone talking about secrets?" Brant asked as he pulled out his chair to sit down.

Lucas looked at the man in chino slacks and a loose white shirt. Bentley's fax on this man had been short and not so sweet. Weston was an investment counselor who made bad investments for his clients and was in a lot of hot water with an old girlfriend. She was claiming date rape when Weston took off. And if he stayed on the ship back to San Francisco, he'd probably be arrested.

"Yes, you did," Lucas said. "We were just saying that each of us must have deep, dark secrets. How about it? What's your secret?"

Brant gave Lucas a cutting look, then glanced at Shelley. "It's no secret that I like pretty women."

"No deep dark secret you're hiding from all of us?" Lucas asked.

Brant shifted in his chair, ignoring the food in front of him. "Don't have a one," he said, then smiled at Shelley and said, "but I do know your little secret, Shelley."

IT'S FUN! IT'S FREE!
AND IT COULD MAKE YOU A
MILLIONAIRE

If you've ever played scratch-off lottery tickets, you should be familiar with how our games work. On each of the first four tickets (numbered 1 to 4 in the upper right) there are Pink Strips to scratch off.

Using a coin, do just that—carefully scratch the PINK strips to reveal how much each ticket could be worth if it is a winning ticket. Tickets could be worth from $100.00 to $1,000,000.00 in lifetime money ($33,333.33 each year for 30 years).

Note, also, that each of your 4 tickets has a unique sweepstakes Lucky Number... and that's 4 chances for a **BIG WIN!**

FREE BOOKS!

At the same time you play your tickets to qualify for big prizes, you are invited to play ticket #5 to get brand-new Harlequin American Romance® novels. These books have a cover price of $3.50 each, but they are yours to keep absolutely free.

There's no catch. You're under no obligation to buy anything. We charge nothing—ZERO—for your first shipment. And you don't have to make any minimum number of purchases—not even one!

The fact is thousands of readers enjoy receiving books by mail from the Harlequin Reader Service®. They like the convenience of home delivery... they like getting the best new novels months before they're available in stores... and they love our discount prices!

We hope that after receiving your free books you'll want to remain a subscriber. But the choice is yours — to continue or cancel, anytime at all! So why not take us up on our invitation, with no risk of any kind. You'll be glad you did!

PLUS A FREE GIFT!

One more thing, when you accept the free books on ticket #5, you are also entitled to play ticket #6, which is GOOD FOR A GREAT GIFT! Like the books, this gift is totally free and yours to keep as thanks for giving our Reader Service a try!

So scratch off the PINK STRIPS on all your BIG WIN tickets and send for everything today! You've got nothing to lose and everything to gain!

Here are your BIG WIN Game Tickets potentially worth from $100.00 to $1,000,000.00 each. Scratch off the PINK STRIP on each of your Sweepstakes tickets to see what you could win and mail your entry right away. (SEE BACK OF BOOK FOR DETAILS!)

This could be your lucky day - GOOD LUCK!

FOLD AND DETACH ALONG THIS DOTTED LINE—RETURN ALL GAME TICKETS INTACT.

TICKET 1
Scratch PINK STRIP to reveal potential value of cash prize if the sweepstakes number on this ticket is a winning number. Return all game tickets intact.

LUCKY NUMBER

20 985897

TICKET 2
Scratch PINK STRIP to reveal potential value of cash prize if the sweepstakes number on this ticket is a winning number. Return all game tickets intact.

LUCKY NUMBER

7H 985897

TICKET 3
Scratch PINK STRIP to reveal potential value of cash prize if the sweepstakes number on this ticket is a winning number. Return all game tickets intact.

LUCKY NUMBER

6S 985897

TICKET 4
Scratch PINK STRIP to reveal potential value of cash prize if the sweepstakes number on this ticket is a winning number. Return all game tickets intact.

LUCKY NUMBER

4W 985897

TICKET 5
We're giving away brand new books to selected individuals. Scratch PINK STRIP for number of free books you will receive.

AUTHORIZATION CODE

130107-742

TICKET 6
We have an outstanding added gift for you if you are accepting our free books. Scratch PINK STRIP to reveal gift.

AUTHORIZATION CODE

130107-742

YES!
Enter my Lucky Numbers in The Million Dollar Sweepstakes (III) and when winners are selected, tell me if I've won any prize. If the PINK STRIP is scratched off on ticket #5, I will also receive four FREE Harlequin American Romance® novels along with the FREE GIFT on ticket #6, as explained on the back and on the opposite page. 154 CIH ANT2 (U-H-AR-07/94)

NAME _____

ADDRESS _____ APT. _____

CITY _____ STATE _____ ZIP CODE _____

Book offer limited to one per household and not valid to current Harlequin American Romance® subscribers. All orders subject to approval.

THE HARLEQUIN READER SERVICE®: HERE'S HOW IT WORKS

Accepting free books places you under no obligation to buy anything. You may keep the books and gift and return the shipping statement marked "cancel". If you do not cancel, about a month later we will send you 4 additional novels, and bill you just $2.89 each plus 25¢ delivery and applicable sales tax, if any.* That's the complete price, and—compared to cover prices of $3.50 each—quite a bargain! You may cancel at any time, but if you choose to continue, every month we'll send you 4 more books, which you may either purchase at the discount price...or return at our expense and cancel your subscription.

* Terms and prices subject to change without notice. Sales tax applicable in N.Y.

For the past several minutes, Shelley had been fighting the urge to look right at Lucas. But self-preservation had made her concentrate on Emily. She knew if she met his gaze, the tingling awareness that had haunted her since the moment she looked up at the swimming lesson would be there. And heaven help her, but she wasn't at all sure how to deal with it.

But Brant Weston was another matter. He had an uncanny similarity to Rob, her ex-husband, and she wouldn't be fooled by that sort again. He was easy to deal with, but right now, his words jarred her. "What?"

He stared at her. "You're dying to get to know me."

She exhaled with real relief. "You don't know a thing about me," she murmured, capable of keeping ahead of a man who was disagreeable at best.

Brant arched one eyebrow at her, then his gaze slipped past her to Emily. "I know this must be your kid."

"I'm Emily Sarah Kingston," Emily said.

"Ah, I was right," he said as he fingered his glass of juice. The smile came again, and it was every bit as grating as it had been at first. "I'd love to take your beautiful mother into Ensenada today." He looked at Shelley. "How about it?"

Thankfully Lillian cut in. "We were just talking about Shelley and Emily coming with us. We're getting a group together to make a day of it."

She hadn't been paying much attention at the buffet table when Lillian and Jessie had asked her, but right now she could have kissed Lillian. "I was just about to tell you we'd love to come along."

"But, Mommy, I'm supposed to be going to that party with Martha," Emily said quickly. "It's going to be really fun, and they said that we're going to get to make wishes on the Christmas tree and..." Her voice trailed off. "I wanted to go, Mommy."

"I know, but that was before I thought about going to Ensenada."

"But you said—"

"I know, but if I leave the ship, I don't want to leave you on board."

"But I'll be with Martha."

Shelley looked at Lucas over Emily's head, but he was looking at Emily, not her.

"Mommy, I'll be real good, and I'll be real careful, and if any bad pers—"

Lucas cut off Emily's words by saying, "I think you need to talk to your mother later about this." He looked at Emily, getting her full attention before she could say anything else. "Don't you think so, Emily?"

"I... guess so," she said quietly.

"If you can come we'd love it, but if you can't come, Emily, we'll do something together later on," Lillian said. "The professor's agreed to come along." She looked at Lucas. "How about you, Mr. Jordon, would you like to accompany us?"

"What time are you leaving?"

"Around eleven."

"I'll be there," he said.

"Mr. Weston? How about you?"

"Count me out," he muttered. "I'm not much for group tours and activities."

"Oh, we'll miss you," Lillian said without much conviction. "But the rest of us will just have to carry on."

"Yes, we will," Shelley said without looking at Brant.

Emily pulled on her sleeve, and when she leaned down, Emily whispered, "Mr. Weston's impudent, isn't he, Mommy?"

"You're very perceptive," she said softly.

Emily nodded solemnly, then said, "Can we go?"

Shelley looked at Emily's partially eaten food. "Did you get enough food?"

"Lots, besides, Martha says that they'll have a lot of stuff at the party..." She shrugged. "If I go."

"All right. We'll go down now. I need to make a few calls before going to Ensenada." She looked at Lillian and Jessie. "Where should we all meet?"

"Right where the ship-to-shore launch loads. You can't miss it."

Chapter Eight

Shelley could sense Lucas close behind her as they stepped on deck in the warming sunlight. Chancing a glance to her left, she saw him fall into step beside Emily as they headed toward the elevators. The clear sunlight was uncompromising in the way it exposed his features.

Rugged wasn't quite the right word for him, but there was nothing delicate about the man, either. He seemed large, almost roughly hewn, yet the planes and angles of his profile were disturbingly male. She looked ahead of them, touching her tongue to lips that were a bit dry.

Emily skipped to keep up and spoke to Lucas. "Lucas, will you tell Mommy to let me go to the party?"

"That's up to her. You're her daughter."

"But she listens to you. She doesn't listen to a lot of people, but she listens to you."

Shelley stared straight ahead, but she knew Lucas was looking at her. "Oh, does she?"

"Yes, she does, and if you tell her, she'll let me go with Martha."

"It's her decision," he said.

But he was neatly backing her into a corner by leaving it all up to her, she thought. There was no way he could understand her hesitancy at being separated from Emily if there was any chance they were in danger. "I just don't like being that far from Emily," she admitted quietly.

"I'll be real good, real, real good, and I promise I'll do everything Martha says to do. And she's nice, Mommy, she's real nice. Please can I go?"

Lucas glanced at Shelley. "I think she understands the situation. Besides, we're no more than five minutes away by the launch. Martha knows who to contact, what to do, if there's any trouble at all."

Shelley exhaled, hesitant to agree, but at a loss to put up any more arguments. "All right. But we'll only stay in Ensenada for an hour or so, agreed?"

"Agreed," he said.

Emily smiled up at the two adults. "See, Lucas, she listens to you. It's because you're a cop."

"I don't think that's quite it, Emily."

Emily frowned. "Do you have something?"

He didn't stop walking as he glanced at her. "What?"

"Are you sick or something?"

Shelley knew Emily had seen Lucas's shoulder, but she hadn't said anything about it. She just hoped that the child wouldn't bring that up. "Not recently, why?"

"Are you giving Mommy something?" she said as they stopped at the elevator.

"Emily, what are you talking about?" Shelley asked.

Emily looked at Shelley. "Miss Lillian said that Lucas was really catching to you."

Shelley stared at her daughter, not chancing a look at Lucas. Damn the heat in her face and her inability to come up with some casual answer for Emily. "When did she say that?" Lucas asked.

"When she was talking to Miss Jessie," the child said, looking remarkably tiny next to the tall man who was pressing the down button for the elevator. "What does it mean?"

"It's an old saying," Shelley said quickly as Emily turned lavender eyes to her. "She probably said he's quite a catch."

"Yeah, that's it. What's an old saying?"

"It's a way of saying things that people keep using over and over again over the years until everyone uses it and knows what it means."

That garbled explanation just confused Emily more, and when Shelley saw her crinkle up her nose, she knew that another question was on the way. Thankfully the elevator doors opened right then, and when Shelley would have urged Emily to get on, someone said, "What luck!"

Shelley looked up at Martha stepping off the elevator, a red and green outfit of stretch pants and sweater looking garishly seasonal. "Martha," she said with great relief. "We were just on our way down to the cabin."

"Well, I was just down there looking for the two of you. They're having an ornament-making class before the party, and I thought Emily might like to do that, too. Something special to make and take home with her."

"Ornaments?" the child asked. "You mean like balls and snowmen and angels you hang on a Christmas tree?"

"That's it," Martha said. "Want to come with me?"

Emily looked at Shelley without saying a word.

"Oh, all right, but you have to change—"

"She doesn't have to change," Martha said. "She looks just fine. It's casual."

"We were thinking of going ashore in Ensenada," Shelley said.

Martha nodded. "You'll love it. It's a wonderful place to get souvenirs and have good food." She smiled down at Emily. "Ready to go and make snowflakes and glitter balls?"

"I sure am, Martha." Emily smiled at Shelley. "Thanks," she said, then took Martha's hand, and as they started down the deck, she waved over her shoulder and called, "Bye."

"So, I'm a catch for you?" Lucas murmured so close to Shelley that it startled her.

She turned and backed up as she looked at him no more than foot from her. "Lillian sounds as if she's got a sideline in matchmaking." She shook her head. "If she only knew."

The doors on the elevator had closed, and Lucas pushed the down button again. "If she knew what?"

She cast him a sidelong glance, and the impact of his gaze when she met it made her tighten. "That you dislike just about everything about me," she said.

"Is that what you think?"

"*You* think I'm some bleeding-heart liberal who sets mad felons loose on society."

The doors slid open, but this time the car was empty and there was no reprieve for Shelley. Lucas touched her in the small of her back to urge her into the car, and she jerked forward, breaking the contact as quickly as she could. As she turned toward the doors inside the car, Lucas stepped in facing her. Without looking away from her, he reached to his right and pushed the floor button, touching the number for their deck.

She'd never much cared what people thought of her, but right now she wished that she knew exactly where she stood with this man. "Well?" Shelley asked as the doors slid shut and the silence between them began to be almost painful to her nerves. "Isn't that what you think?"

He shrugged sharply. "What difference does it make what I think?"

For some reason it made a great difference to her what he thought. "You're protecting me, so your opinion makes a big difference," she said as the car started down.

"Actually, I don't have to agree with, approve of or even like anyone I am assigned to protect."

She looked away at the flashing floor light over Lucas's head. "I guess that's true enough."

"Do you like all your clients?"

She exhaled with a sigh. "I thought we'd gone through this little discussion before."

''We have, and something tells me that we'll do it over and over again.''

Shelley was thankful when the car stopped and the doors opened. Lucas stepped out of the car and she followed, walking past him to start down the corridor without waiting to see if he was following. But she needn't have let it cross her mind. In an instant Lucas was by her side, so close she could feel heat and energy radiating from him, yet far enough away that there was absolutely no physical contact.

Silently she opened her cabin door and stepped back to let Lucas go in ahead of her to check the inside. As he turned and motioned it was all right, she stepped in and closed the door. ''What now?'' she asked.

He glanced at the wall clock. ''We've got an hour. That gives us time to do a few things. Didn't you tell Emily that you needed to make some calls?''

She'd completely forgotten. ''I do. I've got this case that...'' Her voice trailed off. Lucas was the last person she should be talking to about the Moran case. ''I need to check with my office.''

''Just don't let anyone there know where you are.''

''I won't, although I can't conceive of anyone I know there tormenting me like this.''

''Why not?''

''They're friends, colleagues, people who do the same work I do. Why would they be angry or resentful or infuriated by what I do?''

Lucas studied her for a long moment. ''They're human beings. Maybe it's someone who's jealous of what you've accomplished. Did you think of that?''

She had to admit that it had never crossed her mind. "That doesn't make sense."

"Why not?"

"I'm on the bottom rung of the ladder. God, I worked for years to get through law school, to get this far, and it's just the beginning."

"The beginning of what?"

"My career. That's why I'm doing this. I needed to get credentials, and if I can make it big in the PD's office, I can petition some of the best firms in the city."

"That's what this is to you? How far and how high you can go?"

He looked furious, and she wasn't at all sure why. "It's my career."

"And being a PD is a career move, a way to get to the big money?"

"It's a way for me to give Emily some security without having to depend on anyone else."

No matter what she said, it only seemed to make him more angry. "No matter what it costs?"

"I don't understand."

He came closer, and his hand cupped her chin with no gentleness, yet without any pain. She was forced to look right into his dark eyes. "The psycho who's after you doesn't see it as your job. They see it as some perversion of justice. You see it as simply a stepping-stone on the way up in your grand career."

Maybe she understood, after all. "Is that what you really think?" she whispered.

"I guess I do."

"You're very wrong," she whispered, his fingers branding her skin and making her voice sound vaguely hoarse.

"Am I?"

"Yes, you are. You don't understand at all."

His hold on her tightened a fraction, and she made herself stand very still. "You're right," he said, surprising her. "I don't understand a lot of things anymore."

"Like what?"

He stared at her, then slowly he shifted, cupping her face between his large hands. His eyes flickered with a desire that came to her with flashing wonder. Her tongue darted out to touch her lips, and she barely had time to gasp before he whispered, "I don't understand this," and his mouth slanted over hers.

If the first kiss had been riveting for her, this kiss was shattering. It sent a tremor through her, tumbling across her nerves and tightening her soul.

Before she had time to recognize her intent, her arms went around his neck, and she arched toward him. She hadn't meant to return the caress. She hadn't meant to open her lips, inviting his onslaught. She hadn't meant to be this needy, either. It was shattering to her, but her whole body strained toward him, and when his hold on her shifted until she was locked in his strong embrace, she knew that she hadn't meant to let any man get this close to her again.

His hands ran down her back, skimming over her thin cotton dress, yet the contact was as potent as if it had been skin to skin. Her breasts swelled against his chest, and she felt a heaviness growing in her that she ached to relieve. Sinking her fingers in his thick hair, she met his kiss with passion, relishing his tongue tasting her and welcoming his invasion.

She moaned as his hand pressed at the small of her back, bringing her unflinchingly against the evidence of his desire, and need shifted to obsession. She wanted him. She needed him. Despite what he thought of her, she knew that she was finding something in him that had no name but was a living, fundamental need. Abandoning all reason seemed rational. Letting whatever happened happen seemed logical.

But when Lucas eased her to the side and they fell onto the bed, tangled together, she suddenly realized that passion was just that, passion. Lust was lust. And despite how she ached to know this man, to have him hold her and love her, it wasn't love. He didn't even like her. A chill started to kill the fire, and when she rolled away from Lucas and managed to get to the edge of the bed and sit there, she knew that she'd settled for much less than perfect love before. She wouldn't again.

She clutched at the straps of her dress that had been pushed aside, and closed her eyes tightly. There were no words, no explanations, and she sat there, silently praying that Lucas would just dissolve into thin air. Then she felt the bed shift, and the next thing she knew, she heard a door click open. Then the door closed and silence surrounded her.

She didn't have to turn and look to see if Lucas was gone. She could feel the emptiness as surely as she could feel the ache of frustration in her whole body.

THE *RIO DEL SOL* was long and sleek, a gleaming white ship against the true blue of the ocean and the paleness of the clear winter sky. As the ship-to-shore launch approached Ensenada, a city stretched out lazily in either direction, sunlight glinted off windows and tile roofs. The docking area was crowded with vessels from other ships anchored off the shore, and small boats had come in to dock.

Shelley sat between the professor and Lillian, and she didn't look at Lucas on the other side of Jessie. She didn't want to be close to him, not even on a crowded ship-to-shore boat. She didn't want him to touch her again, not on purpose or even accidentally. She gripped her leather shoulder bag tightly and stared at the city as it got closer and closer.

"I heard about a restaurant on the street near the docks that has wonderful food," Lillian said. "I suppose good Mexican food in Mexico is a bit of overkill, but a nice lady on the ship told me not to miss this place."

"What's it called?" Shelley asked without looking at Lillian, her eyes traveling over rows of shops that lined the streets by the docks.

"Dos Gringos."

She glanced at the lady. "I don't know much Spanish, but doesn't that mean two people who aren't Mexican?"

"Exactly, my dear," the professor said. "A gimmick, to be sure."

"That doesn't mean the food won't be quite lovely," Lillian persisted. "The lady I talked to was quite knowledgeable. She's been here several times."

The professor glanced at Lillian with a smile. "Of course, my dear. Of course. We will most certainly stop there for our meal before coming back to the ship." He looked past Lillian and Shelley. "That is if it's all right with everyone."

Shelley heard Lucas say, "It's fine with me."

Jessie agreed. "Lovely, just lovely."

"Then it's settled," Lillian said. "And here we are."

As the boat glided to a stop by a dock that led up to a myriad of single-story shops and buildings, a voice came over the loudspeaker. "The ship-to-shore runs at the top of every hour until six o'clock, then it's by special request. Have a pleasant day in Ensenada."

Shelley got up and followed Lillian and the professor up the short walkway to the dock. The day was warm, in the seventies, and the air held the aromas of cinnamon, coffee and the ocean. She inhaled deeply. The moments in the cabin an hour ago were, thankfully, a fading memory. She adjusted her purse on her shoulder and smiled at Lillian. "What a great idea to come here."

"It's part of the cruise," Lillian said. "I didn't think we should miss it. And it's quite nice to get off the ship for a while, too."

Shelley walked off the dock onto the cobbled street, and by the time they got to the main street of the town, she was able to act almost normal when Lucas came up by her side and looked down at her.

She couldn't smile or act casual, but she could at least meet his gaze and not miss her step. He'd changed into Levi's and a plain white shirt, and the light breeze ruffled his dark hair. When he fell into step with the professor as they started looking through the shops, she moved closer to Lillian and Jessie. When they stopped for lunch at the restaurant Lillian had heard about, Shelley actually started to feel in control. A distinct contrast to her actions in the cabin earlier.

They got a table outside the old adobe building in a tiled courtyard shaded by olive trees and overlooking the harbor. Shelley could see their ship riding out past the breakers, gleaming in the sunlight, and other ships anchored near the *Rio Del Sol*. A bag of souvenirs rested on the tiles near her feet with her purse, and she cradled a cool glass filled with a tart margarita in her hands.

After they finished their lunch, she pushed away her almost empty plate and sank back in her chair. "That was wonderful food," she said.

"My friend certainly knew what she was talking about," Lillian said as she finished off the last of her caramelized flan. "Simply delicious." She looked at Lucas and the professor across the table. They had been eating in relative silence. "How about you gentlemen, was the food to your liking?"

"Very much so," the professor said.

Lucas sat back in his chair. "It was good."

Lillian checked her watch. "We really should get going or we'll have another hour to wait for the next ship-to-shore boat."

As Shelley put in her money, she chanced a look at Lucas. She was relieved to find him counting out money for the bill and not looking at her. When they all stood and started for the docking area, Shelley fell into step beside Lillian although she was very aware of Lucas right behind her. The streets were crowded with people, most of whom were coming up from the docking area, and she was jostled from time to time.

As they approached the cobbled street that led to the docking area, Shelley and Lillian cut through the press of people to get to the crossing lights. She stopped at the edge of the curb, waiting for the light to change, and saw a street clock that showed five minutes to the hour. If they hurried they could make the launch.

She was anxious to see Emily, to find out what she'd been doing, and she needed to get away from Lucas for awhile. The air seemed to vibrate with his presence when he was anywhere in her vicinity, and she was exhausted from the effort of trying to act as if she didn't care he was close to her.

She could feel people behind her and around her, at her sides and at her back. And she didn't have to turn to know that Lucas was there, his proximity building an intensity in her that made her uneasy. But she wouldn't look. As she stared determinedly at the red light, she was jarred as someone struck her elbow with their arm. She stumbled slightly, then caught herself, and the next instant, she felt a blow in the middle of her back.

The sheer force of impact pitched her forward and sent her tumbling uncontrollably out into the street. Frantically, she tried to stop herself, but she was helpless to keep from falling onto the cobbles. Horns blared, tires screeched and engines roared and she hit the ground with the flat of her hands, the jarring stop ricocheting through her body.

Awkwardly, she pushed up and twisted, confused and disoriented, then she saw movement, a bus coming right at her. Terror choked her, and she knew she didn't have time to get out of the way before the bus struck her.

For a moment Lucas thought Shelley was jumping off the curb to cross the street against the light. He turned, reaching with his right hand to stop her, then he realized that she was out of control, pitching toward the cobbled pavement. Her purse and bag went flying as she struck the cobbles, pushed back, then turned, and a city bus was bearing down on her.

Raw fear sent a painful surge of adrenaline through him, and he acted instinctively. He lunged toward Shelley, grabbed her and shoved her as hard as he could away from the curb and the bus. Miraculously, they both ended up in the middle of the street. When he hit the pavement with his left shoulder, pain seared through him, but he held Shelley tightly with his right arm, and the bus was passing by. It was close enough to make a rush of hot air at his back, but it didn't touch either one of them.

There was a blur of people all around, their voices raised in shouts, and confusion everywhere, but all Lucas was aware of was Shelley lying half under him. The heat of her gasping breaths brushed his face, and he could feel her heart pounding against his. Then hands were on him, tugging him upward, and Shelley was being helped to her feet.

He was on his feet facing Shelley, who was holding to Lillian's arm for support. Her hair was loose, tangled around her pale face, and her white dress was stained with tar and dirt. But she was standing facing him, shaken but whole, yet the fear lingered in him. She could have been hit by the bus, and the idea of that happening was making him feel nauseated.

How could he have let down his guard so completely? Why had he let the memory of that kiss drive him to keep a distance from her instead of being right by her? He cursed himself for the mistakes he'd made. He should have been aware of everything, even someone tripping on the curb.

Regret mingled with relief as he reached out to touch her, needing to feel her vitality. He brushed the tips of his fingers along her soiled cheek and could feel her trembling. "Are you all right?"

Her tongue darted out to touch her pale lips. "I...I think so," she said as she looked past him at the pressing crowd that surrounded them.

He let his hand drop to her shoulder when he really wanted to pull her to him and hold on for dear life. It unnerved him when she reached up and covered his hand with hers. But she wasn't looking at him. She was scanning the crowds, her hand tightening more and more where it covered his.

Lillian and Jessie hovered by her side, the two of them clutching her purse and bag, their faces ashen, their expressions filled with concern. And the professor was behind, looking as if he was in shock. Lucas caught a glimpse of Brant Weston on the outside fringe of the gathering crowds, staring at them. The newlyweds were in the center of the crowd, just watching. Then the sound of sirens cut through the air, startling Shelley. She looked at Lucas, the deep lavender of her eyes vivid against the paleness of her complexion.

"Please, can we leave?" she asked.

Lucas looked around at the police cars careening down the street in their direction, and he knew that getting involved with the local authorities even for an accident could be a mistake.

"Sure," he said to Shelley, then spoke to Lillian and Jessie. "Let's get her back to the ship where the doctor can check her."

"Is it wise to move her too much?" Lillian asked.

"Very wise," Lucas said, and taking Shelley by the arm, he started through the crowd. They broke out of the ring of people, and didn't stop until they were on the dock. He heard shouts from behind him in Spanish, but didn't stop. He took Shelley with him up the stairs, into the milling crowd that was waiting for several launches that serviced the ships beyond the breakwater.

In seconds they were swallowed up, and when he finally stopped by the pickup point for their launch, he saw the sleek vessel just casting off to head for the ship. "Damn it," he muttered, and led Shelley to an empty space on one of several benches built into the dock under the shade of lattice canopies.

Shelley sank down onto the closest wooden seat with one look around to make sure the police weren't on their way. Lucas sat next to her. One look at her pale face and the dirt smudging her dress, and he finally let himself do what he'd wanted to from the first. He slipped his arm around her and drew her close to him.

Chapter Nine

Shelley stiffened for a split second, then with a sigh she almost collapsed against Lucas, her cheek pressed to the hollow of his shoulder. The cool, contained realist was scared to death. So was he. And he hurt so badly that the pain had gone beyond simple discomfort to something he could only call torment. But it didn't come close to the intensity of his fear when he relived the image of Shelley plunging in front of that bus.

"That was terrifying," Lillian said as she sat down on the other side of Shelley. "Just terrifying."

"You're a hero, Mr. Jordon," Jessie said as she stopped by Lucas. "You saved the dear girl's life. That bus would have surely..." She shuddered expressively. "You are a hero."

"I just did what anyone would have done," Lucas murmured.

The professor stopped beside Jessie. "You acted above and beyond the call, dear man. That bus couldn't have stopped in time. And in this country, goodness knows who they would have thought was at fault."

"Well, it's over," Lucas murmured, bent on not reliving that moment again, but his hold on Shelley tightened. "And everything's all right."

"You really should see the ship doctor when we get back on board," Lillian said to Shelley. "But the launch just left, and there won't be another run for an hour."

Jessie spoke up. "Maybe we could contact the ship and have them send the launch back for us right away. The man on the loudspeaker mentioned something about special request for trips. I think this is special enough. Shelley shouldn't have to sit out here for an hour after what happened, and they're supposed to put the welfare and comfort of the passenger first and foremost."

"This is certainly an emergency," the professor said. "I shall be happy to go and make that call. I will insist that they send the launch back."

"I'll come along with you," Jessie said.

"I will, too." Lillian stood. "Maybe if we all put in our request, they'll be more inclined to cooperate."

As the three of them headed toward the nearest shop to call, Lucas felt Shelley lay her hand on his forearm.

"Lucas?"

He ignored the pain that blazed through his left side. "It's all right. It's over." Words said to comfort her couldn't minimize that moment in his memory when he saw her in front of the bus. The idea of her being hurt terrified him. "It was an accident," he whispered. "You stumbled or tripped, but it's over."

Her hand on his arm tightened, her fingers pressing into his forearm, and pain shot through him. He inhaled and tried to shift away from the hold. "Shelley, please, don't do that."

She jerked back, her eyes huge, and she whispered, "I'm sorry. You're hurt."

"Just bruised," he said, hating the feeling of emptiness produced by her retreating from his hold on her.

"Lucas, when I was on the curb, I felt something, a hand at my back." He could see real fear in her lavender eyes as she breathed. "Someone pushed me in front of the bus."

Despite the heat of the sun, Shelley felt a distinct cold rush that could have come from a sudden cool breeze or from the sickening, wrenching feeling of knowing that someone had tried to kill her.

"What?" Lucas asked as he shifted and caught her by her shoulder with his right hand to square her with him.

She looked into the intensity of his dark eyes and could barely form the words. "Someone pushed me."

His fingers dug into her shoulders. "You saw someone?"

She shook her head. "No, I felt someone close, near my back." She couldn't tell him she thought it was him, that she was sensing his body heat and closeness, or how disoriented that made her feel. "Then someone bumped me, and the next thing I knew, someone hit my back."

His breath was released in a low hiss. "Are you sure?"

She couldn't forget that feeling of someone behind her, someone close, or the intensity she could feel in that person. "I felt it. I..." The impact of the hand on her back was burned in her mind, and she hated that sense of vulnerability it brought with it. She hated feeling as if she was exposed, that someone could be close by, watching her with Lucas, cursing the fact she wasn't laying dead on the cobbled road.

"It couldn't have been an accident, someone tripping or impatient to get through the crowd?"

"I...I guess. It happened so fast...just a push and the bus..."

She couldn't control an involuntary shudder. Lucas's hold on her tightened. "Shelley, listen to me," he said in a low voice. "If you really were pushed, this is just the start."

"Of what?" She barely managed to breathe.

"Whoever's been threatening you, notes and calls aren't enough now. Maybe it's because you took off, but it escalated his obsession and his threat to you."

"This was Bentley's idea," she muttered "I didn't want to run. He thought I should. That I should get out of the city, onto neutral ground."

"Listen to me. Bentley didn't know the person could get to you here. He didn't know they could find out where you went. If you were pushed, they know exactly where you are, and the odds are pretty good that they're close by now."

"But I didn't tell anyone where we were going. I was so careful."

"Obsessive people are particularly cunning. It comes with the territory. Trust me, it wouldn't really

matter where you hid out. Sooner or later, it would
have happened. This just put it on fast forward." His
dark eyes scanned the area as he talked to her. "The
bottom line is we need to tighten security and form a
new strategy."

"A strategy?"

His gaze came to meet hers. "From now on this is
the way it is. No more shore excursions. No more distance between us. We're going to stay on the ship, and
stay together. Period."

There was obviously no room for discussion with
him, but Shelley had no idea how she could maintain
any semblance of emotional stability if she couldn't
put some distance between herself and this man.
"Maybe we should just get off the ship and fly back
to the city."

"If you want to, do it. You're not a prisoner. It's
your choice, but you'll be giving the person carte
blanche to come at you from a million angles in the
city. If you stay on the ship, everything's restricted.
People, access, places. Go back and you'll be looking
over your shoulder every minute of the day, or stay on
the ship and limit the person's options. It's up to you."

He let her go but didn't move back, and she hated
the feeling of isolation that was overtaking her. She
clutched her hands so tightly in her lap that her nails
dug into her palms. "What would you do if you were
me?" she asked Lucas.

He regarded her with narrowed eyes. "That doesn't
matter. It's your life. It's your call."

"It's not just my life. It's Emily's, too."

"I told Bentley to get the child out of it, to send her to a relative's, but he said that wouldn't work. What about your ex-husband? Surely if he knew what was going on, he'd take Emily in a minute."

If she could have laughed, she would have. But she knew if she tried, she'd probably cry. "Rob isn't an option in any of this, so forget about him."

"What about grandparents?"

"No."

"A friend?"

She shook her head. "There isn't anyone close enough to ask."

Unexpectedly he cupped her chin in the heat of his right hand and came even closer to her. "You're really on your own, aren't you?"

"I have been for a long time," she murmured, and for the first time in what seemed forever, she wished it wasn't just her and Emily. If things could be different, if there was someone she could go to, and hold, and lean on, she knew she'd grab it with both hands. But as she looked at Lucas, she knew that what she really wished was for him to be that person.

The thought jolted her, and she drew back from his touch. She knew what she had to do. "We'll stay on the ship for now, at least until we reach Cabo San Lucas."

He exhaled in a rush. "All right. That's settled. Now, there's more rules."

"Go ahead."

"We're not to be apart at all. As far as everyone on board knows, we met, and it was fate. We'll make the newlyweds look like strangers."

She stared at him with horror. "That's crazy."

"What's crazy? You're a beautiful woman. I'm passable for a man. We're both free. We met and bingo, instant attraction. Is it too improbable to think that we could fall in love?"

The question hung between them, and Shelley realized an instant truth. It would be remarkably easy for her to fall in love with Lucas, differences and all. But she wouldn't. She'd plunged in once, following her hormones, and heaven knew this man made her hormones go crazy, but the only good thing that came out of her past foolishness was Emily. "Whatever you want, we'll do it. Just tell me what you want me to do."

"Don't say anything about this not being an accident." He spoke as he looked past her. "The sisters and the professor are heading back this way, so let them go on thinking you stumbled. We need every advantage we can get right now."

The idea of the professor or the sisters being involved in anything like this was unthinkable to her. "Lucas, you can't think..."

"Well, I do," he murmured, then spoke past her. "Any luck?"

"Yes, success!" the professor said.

Shelley turned and saw the sisters and the professor nearing the bench. "They're happy to send the launch back right away," Lillian said. "They said it wouldn't be longer than ten minutes." She looked down at Shelley. "We'll get you back to the ship and get you cleaned up before you know it."

"I really appreciate everything you've done," Shelley said, unable to picture any of the three people as threats to her.

"It's a shame that you tripped like that," the professor murmured.

"It looked as if you were jumping in front of the bus," Jessie said.

They looked sincerely concerned. Shelley stood and was taken aback when Lucas got up and put his arm around her shoulders, drawing her against his side. "It scared the hell out of me," he murmured.

Jessie looked from Lucas to Shelley, and the hint of a smile touched the corners of her mouth. "Well, I do believe that Mr. Jordon is very concerned about you."

Shelley stayed by Lucas, but she couldn't let herself put her arm around his waist or lean against him. If she did, she might never let go. "*I* was very concerned about me," she said.

"Well, everything is all right now." The professor stopped and turned to look in the direction of an engine noise that was coming closer. "Ah, the launch. Here it comes," he said as he looked at Shelley. "Let's get you back to the ship."

She looked at him, and the idea that he might have been the one to try and hurt her was almost ludicrous. Then Lucas's hold on her tightened just a bit, and she realized that there was no one she could trust here . . . except Lucas. "Yes, back to the ship," she murmured and let Lucas lead her toward the launch.

Even when they had to go single file up the ramp to get aboard, she felt Lucas right behind her, one of his hands resting lightly on her shoulder. And despite all of her conflicting emotions, she relished that bond, that knowledge that he was close by.

While the launch skimmed over the crystal clear water, Shelley kept silent, watching the anchored ship getting closer and closer until they were at the bottom of the stairs. She went first up onto the deck, then turned and almost ran into Lucas behind her. His hand on her shoulder steadied her, then Lillian was by her side.

"Dear, let me take you down to your cabin."

Lucas shocked Shelley by dipping his head to touch his lips to her forehead. The contact was chaste and surely for effect for the others, but the warm caress was almost healing for her. The fear she'd felt before, that sense of vulnerability seemed to be diminishing just a bit, then Lucas drew back and she was pinned by his dark eyes. "I'll take her down to her cabin. Don't worry about her."

"Why, yes, of course," Lillian said. "Will you be feeling up to coming to dinner this evening, Shelley?"

"I ... I don't know."

"I hope you feel up to it, and that you bring Emily. She's a wonderful child." She handed Shelley her purse and bag. "Just wonderful."

Lucas put his arm around Shelley. "We'll see how she feels later."

The sisters and the professor made their goodbyes, and Shelley and Lucas headed for the elevators. Lucas didn't let go of her. The contact stayed intact until the doors to the elevator closed, then Shelley tested it by leaning away, and Lucas let her go. She touched the wall with her hand and she welcomed the coolness of the mirrored panel against her palm. Staring at the closed doors as the elevator started down, she said, "Do you really think the person who's after me is someone we've met on the ship?"

"It could be."

She met his gaze in the distorted reflection of the elevator doors. "But the professor and the sisters..."

"It's easier to imagine someone like Sloan or Weston, isn't it?"

"Well, I guess it is."

"That's your mistake, one I wouldn't have thought you'd make."

"What mistake?"

"Thinking someone threatening you or pushing you in front of a bus has to look like a criminal. You've dealt with enough people to know it doesn't make a tinker's damn of difference what a person looks like. Serial killers can look like Sunday school teachers, and drug dealers look like upscale yuppies." She watched him turn to her, but she kept her eyes on their reflections in the doors. "But maybe that's your fatal flaw."

That brought her head around, and she met his eyes directly. "What are you talking about?"

"Misjudging people. It must make it easier for you to represent some of the people you get off."

It always came back to that, and it made Shelley feel depressed rather than mad now. "I'm not going into that right now."

"You're right. It doesn't do a bit of good, does it?"

She turned from him as the doors opened, and before he could say anything else, she was out of the car and starting down the hallway. When he caught up to her, he gripped her upper arm, but she didn't stop as she tried to break free of the contact. She knew it was futile to fight his hold on her as she kept going, and she was grateful when they got to the door to her cabin.

But Lucas still didn't let her go. With his free hand, he reached for her key and opened the door. He leaned into the cabin, looked around, then moved forward, pulling her inside with him. The cabin was empty as Lucas swung the door shut with a resounding crack. Finally he let her go, but before she could walk away from him, he was right in front of her, blocking her escape route with his body.

Inches from her, she could feel tension in him, and she wasn't entirely certain if it came from anger at her or what had happened on shore. "What now?" she asked, clenching her hands into fists at her side.

He exhaled with a hiss, and she could feel the heat of his breath fan her skin. "What does it take to get through to you?"

"About what?"

"I've told you to stay close to me, to never walk away from me like you just tried to at the elevator."

"I'm not going to stand there and let you do that to me."

"Do what?"

"Attack everything I do."

"I don't."

"You do. You haven't let me forget for one minute that you hate what I do."

He looked taken aback, but he didn't move. "Hate's a pretty strong word."

"Is it the wrong word?"

He hesitated. "I think it is. In fact, as strange as this sounds, I can almost see the logic in it all."

She was stunned. "What?"

"Does that surprise you that I can think things over and see a different slant on things?"

"Are you serious?"

He sighed, an almost weary sigh. "Take what I'm offering, because this doesn't happen very often. Just about as often as I apologize to someone."

"You can see that I don't define the boundaries of my job? That the law does?"

"Actually, I can see that. It's the same way with my job. It's down in black and white, the rules."

"Yes, rules," she murmured. "They're fixed, no matter what we do. When I defend the guilty and they get convicted, it's a good conviction. It's not going to be overturned or set aside in an appeals court."

"And when you know you set a guilty person free?" he asked softly.

She closed her eyes for a moment, then braced herself and looked at Lucas. "I hate it," she admitted.

"Like Freddy Monroe?"

"I had no idea. But his arrest was bad. I didn't do that."

"Why did you go to the funeral?"

She shook her head. "I don't know. I felt as if I had to, but there wasn't any logic behind it." She wished she could tell him how it tore her up to know that someone who shouldn't be in prison would be, and someone who deserved it wouldn't be. She tossed her purse and bag onto a chair by the door and murmured, "I wouldn't do it again."

"Why not?"

Finding the words to explain herself to Lucas was getting harder and harder for her, and it didn't help that she almost felt apologetic about her job. "I didn't belong there. I had no business intruding on that grief." She had a startlingly clear image of him in the gray mists. "I don't think I was thinking about guilt or feeling responsible, but it's painful to see people suffer like that."

He touched his shoulder and massaged it through the thin cotton of his shirt that held smears of dirt from the pavement. "Have you ever wondered before what happened to the people you free?"

"I hear about some of them." It made her sick to think about Freddy Monroe, with his smug face and filthy mouth. But the truth was if she'd let him get sentenced, it would have been overthrown in appeals. And court time would have been eaten up for nothing.

She stared at Lucas, her eyes burning, and she wished she had the words to explain things to him. She felt she was so close to having him understand, having herself understand, but she wasn't quite there. Then the phone shattered the moment, startling her, and when she would have gone to answer it, Lucas moved to it. "I'll get it."

She watched him lift the receiver and say, "Yes?" He listened, then murmured, "Sure thing," then hung up slowly and carefully.

He stared at his hand on the receiver for a long moment, then drew back and turned narrowed eyes on her. Any softness in his expression from moments ago, gone as if it had never been. "A message for you."

"Has something else happened?"

He shook his head, and she felt a vise on her chest release. "No, nothing to do with this case."

Her heart dropped. "God, it's Emily?"

"No, it's a message for you from someone in your office, a Ryan Sullivan."

Her relief left her almost dizzy. "What is it?"

"Bobby Moran walked. The judge gave him supervised probation for three years, part of it served in a halfway house, and he'll have to make restitution to the couple he robbed. He says that you've won a big one."

A victory for her, and her impulse was to tell Lucas, to share it with him. But one look at his closed face stopped her.

"Aren't you pleased?" he asked in a deceptively soft voice.

She slowly sank down on the bed and stared at her hands in her lap. "Bobby Moran isn't a criminal," she breathed.

His sharp laugh jarred her, and she looked up at him. "Robbing someone doesn't make him a criminal?"

She closed her eyes for a moment then looked at Lucas. "Bobby Moran is a poor street kid who's fought tooth and nail to try and be something. He was in the wrong place at the wrong time and got pulled into that robbery. He's not some hard-core criminal, some animal who needs to be locked up. What he needs is another chance, an opportunity to get his life together and make something of himself.''

"Tell that to his victims," Lucas said in an almost flat voice.

Shelley stood abruptly. She'd had enough. After almost making that contact, almost feeling as if there was something there with Lucas, she couldn't bear this closed door. "Who made you omniscient? You're not God."

He studied her hard and long, then shrugged. "I'm not even close to that," he said with a decided weariness in his tone. "I just arrest them."

"Then make sure you do it right," she said, the words almost a plea.

He leaned closer to her. "Listen to me, lady. When someone's in trouble, they call a cop. Next time you need help, call a PD. Or call Ryan whatever-his-name-is. Leave me out of it."

Frustration and anger burned through Shelley, and before she had time to think or reason, she lifted her hand and swung at Lucas. But before she could make contact, he had her by her wrist, and she knew what the action cost him in pain when his lips rimmed with white and dots of moisture shone on his forehead.

His fingers were an imprisoning bracelet on her wrist, and she tried to jerk free. But she was as effective as a moth trying to beat down a brick wall. "Don't you ever think of doing that again," he ground out.

Shelley closed her eyes and said in a tight voice, "Let me go."

Lucas released her with a sharp downward movement, and her hand swung back to strike the footboard of the bed. She gasped and jerked back, gripping her hand to her chest. Before she could look at her knuckles, Lucas had her hand. But this time his touch was gentle as he held her and looked at the redness on her knuckles. He looked up to meet her gaze. "I'm sorry."

The man had gone from angry to gentle in a heartbeat, and she found this version much more difficult to deal with. "Forget it," she murmured.

He ran a finger over her knuckles, and the contact made her tremble. "I never meant to hurt you."

"No matter how much you dislike me?" she whispered.

He looked at her, then with his other hand, he brushed her cheek with the tips of his fingers. "God, you're so far off the mark it's almost laughable."

Moods with this man took tremendous swings, and Shelley could feel the air exploding around them, the electricity of awareness building. "You dislike everything I stand for," she whispered, wishing that words could take away the tension and ease the way Lucas seemed to seep into her soul.

But nothing did. His hand moved to cup her chin, and his gaze dropped to her lips, almost as tantalizing as a kiss could be. "I don't hate you. I don't hate what you stand for. I might not like it, but some things are beyond either one of us," he whispered. "Life takes its twists and turns, and sometimes I think we're just along for the ride."

"That's horribly fatalistic," she whispered. "We can make a difference."

He moved closer. "You've made a difference," he said softly, and she knew he was going to kiss her. But she didn't try to move away or break whatever spell seemed to be forming around them.

She held her breath as his lips touched hers, absorbing the feeling of his heat on her mouth, and instinctively, her lips parted. She could feel Lucas hesitate for a single moment, then he drew her to him, and with her hands caught between them, he surrounded her. The kiss deepened with a rush that took her breath away.

A certain abandonment came with the contact and it came from nowhere to swirl around Shelley and catch her in a whirlwind that threatened to consume her. She welcomed his kiss, the exploration of his tongue and the way his hands held her firmly against him. The evidence of his desire came with as much suddenness, and part of her relished the idea that she could reach this man on such a basic level.

Despite their differences, she knew that with this need there were no barriers. There were no walls of anger or frustration. And she pressed her hands against his chest, feeling his heart race under her palms, and she knew that no matter what their meeting ground was, she wanted this man to hold her and to need her as much as she needed him.

His lips trailed along her jawline to her throat, to a sensitive area just under her ear, and she arched toward him. Awkwardly, she shifted her hands to tug at his shirt, to free it from his waistband and to work her hands under the cotton to feel his heat. Lucas moved back, tugging his shirt off and tossing it behind him, then she was back in his arms, his lips on her skin, and she felt the sleek heat of his back, his muscles flexing.

His hands worked their way under the straps of her dress, pushing them off her shoulders, and the material dropped, exposing her lace-covered breasts. She felt his touch on her, and she swelled, her nipples hardening instinctively, and the moan she heard was her own.

Through the haze of desire, Shelley suddenly heard voices, and they jarred her. Lucas drew back, his eyes burning into hers as she heard Martha say, "Here we are, honey."

Chapter Ten

Quickly, Lucas turned and grabbed his shirt, then reached for Shelley's hand. As the key clicked in the lock, Lucas pulled Shelley to the connecting door. At the same time the door to the suite opened, the two of them slipped through into his cabin.

"Well, that was fun," Martha's voice said from the other cabin. "Wasn't it?"

"Terrific," Emily said.

In the darkened cabin, Lucas let go of Shelley and silently eased the connecting door closed. Then he turned to Shelley, his features blurred by the low light of the room where the heavy curtains shut out the sun. She awkwardly tried to get the top of her dress readjusted, more than a bit embarrassed by what had almost happened.

"I think I need a new rule," he whispered, his voice vaguely hoarse.

As she tugged her straps over on her shoulders, she made herself ask, "What is it?"

"It's a rule for me."

"Do I get to hear it?"

He looked at her for a long moment, then exhaled. "I won't touch you any more than I have to." She could feel heat rising in her cheeks. "It leads to things that are better left undone."

She could almost feel the air getting thinner and the space shrinking. "Like this?"

"Yes." He came closer, filling her with each breath she took. And her first impulse was to run like hell. But she stayed still. "There's something you should know about me."

"What, that you have some sort of physical response to me and you hate yourself for it?"

"No."

"Then what?"

"I always finish what I start. It's a stubbornness in me, or maybe a foolishness, and with this, it could be downright stupidity." He held up a hand and touched her lips with his finger to keep her from speaking.

"I'm smart enough to know that we can't do this. There's nothing for us but a lot of problems. You're into your career and I'm a cop. It's that simple."

But it wasn't. Not when he just had to touch her and she lost all reason. Not when she knew that if he touched her right now, she wouldn't let him go. She wouldn't stop. She'd stay with him until he loved her the way she loved him.

That thought sent a jolt through her, a burning chord of shock that seared her. She tried to deny it, but she knew even as she looked at him, it was as true as the fact that he could never love a person like her.

Lucas looked at Shelley and felt the impact the woman could have on him just by being in the same room with him. And he fought it with every rational thought in his being. He knew that stupidity didn't begin to define what he could do with this woman if he let it happen. He deliberately pushed it aside and made himself speak instead of reaching out to hold her against him again.

"We need to keep this simple. I'm here to protect you and Emily. Period. I've got my life when this ship docks. So do you. So let's make sure we're both around to live them."

Words said with cold rationality sounded hollow in his own ears. His life? What was that life? In stark terms, it was work and more work. The past months had proven to him how empty the other areas of his life were. Now this woman with lavender eyes was so close he only had to reach out and feel what reality could be.

"Exactly," she said in a flat voice. "Keep it simple."

A knock sounded on the connecting door, and he took one last look at Shelley before he forced himself to turn from her. "Yes?"

"Lucas?" Emily called through the closed door, and he had one more reason it would be impossible to be involved with this woman. The child.

He opened the door and Emily was there wearing a garland of holly around her neck and a Santa Claus hat on her head. A miniature Shelley, down to the eye color, he thought.

"Emily, what's going on?" Shelley asked from close by Lucas.

"Oh, Mommy, we had such a great time, and I made some stuff, but it had to dry and Santa said that mine got a ribbon 'cause it was so pretty! And he gave me this hat and lots of stuff and he knew my name. He said that he knew all about me and he . . ."

As she finally got a good look at Shelley, her voice trailed off and her eyes got huge. "What happened?" she finally asked.

Shelley decided on the explanation that Lucas wished he could be certain was the truth. "I tripped on the curb and fell on the road in Ensenada."

Emily came closer. "You hurt yourself?"

"No, I'm not hurt, just dirty, and my dignity is a bit bruised. Now, tell me all about what you did."

"You won't believe it!"

Shelley moved, and Lucas could feel her close to him, then she slipped past without making any contact and crouched in front of her daughter. With a gentle touch she smoothed back errant curls at the child's cheek and smiled. "Whatever it was, you look as if you had a lot of fun."

"We had a great time," Martha said.

Lucas glanced at Martha in the next cabin as she watched Shelley with a slight frown. "You fell, Ms. Kingston?"

"I'm a bit clumsy. I tripped on a curb. How did things go with you and Emily?"

"Terrific. Emily partied hearty."

"I sure did." Emily grabbed Shelley by the hand and almost bounced up and down. "Can you come up to the party room to see what I made? And you can meet the people there. Can you, please, you and Lucas?''

Shelley looked at Lucas without making direct eye contact. It was easier to hide the confusion that churned in her. "Well?"

"Sure."

Emily clapped her hands. "Wow, wait until you see what I made and meet everyone!"

"We'll see it in a bit, but first I need to take a shower and change out of this dress."

The child deflated, but reluctantly nodded. "All right. But hurry." She looked at Lucas. "You hurry, too."

"I will." He looked at Shelley. "I'll contact Bentley."

"I guess he should know."

"Know what?" Emily asked.

Shelley spoke up. "It's not important right now. What is important is me getting my shower so you can show me what you did all day."

"We'll go up in half an hour," Lucas said, and as he swung the connecting door shut, the last thing he saw was Shelley bending to kiss her daughter and Martha saying goodbye.

The image stayed in his mind when he put in the call to Bentley, and after he'd left a message for the man to call him as soon as he could, he hung up and the image was still with him. A gentle touch. A kiss. In some odd way he was almost jealous of the child who could accept that affection so easily. With him it got complicated and confused, yet even thinking about it made his body tense.

He took two more aspirin, then grabbed the red ball from the bedside table and laid down on the bedspread. As he waited for the aspirin to take the edge off the discomfort in his shoulder, he stared at the ceiling and worked the ball. But every sound he heard in the next cabin only reminded him of what he'd almost done.

When the phone rang, he sat up on the side of the bed and lifted the receiver. Bentley was on the other end of the line. "What's going on? Your message sounded important."

"I don't know if it is or not, but it looks as if someone might have tried to get to Shelley when we were on shore in Ensenada. She thinks someone tried to push her in front of a bus."

"She *thinks* someone pushed her?"

"She's not really sure, but it could have been the truth."

"Where in the hell were you?"

Trying to keep my distance from her. "I was there, but not close enough."

"Anything else?"

Something was wrong. "You don't sound very surprised about all of this."

The man hesitated. "I guess I'm not."

Lucas sat straighter, a thought coming to him that knotted his middle. "Is this a setup?"

"What?"

"Staking out the goat for the predator to find so you can shoot the predator?"

"Why would I do that?"

"To save the department's collective butt."

"I told you you've got a cushy job. I meant it. Oh, by the way, I've got something else to add to that list I sent you."

Lucas knew he was being diverted and didn't fight it. At least for now. "What is it?"

"Professor Washburn isn't a professor at all. I just found out that he's a librarian at the university. Before that he worked in a bookstore in the city."

"Why did you just come up with it now?"

"The university computer got a mix-up between him and a Professor Washbourne."

Human error, no doubt. "So, he's a librarian?"

"In the criminal law library on campus. From what I found out, he's pretty sharp on criminal law, almost fanatical."

That didn't fit the man he'd met, but he didn't doubt Bentley's report. "So, on a ship with strangers he plays the part of a mellow college professor?"

"And that's not a crime."

He could hear Emily talking excitedly, and he knew he had to get ready to leave. "If you find out anything else, let me know."

"Of course," Bentley said, then the connection was broken.

As Lucas put the receiver back in the cradle, then found a clean shirt and slipped it on, he fought the idea of being set up. He hated the thought. As he discarded the shirt with the soiled shoulder, he ignored the memories of how it got ruined and why he'd taken it off in the first place. He couldn't afford to let himself remember that too clearly, not now. He needed to think.

As he headed for the door, he made the decision to talk Shelley and Emily into staying in their cabin for dinner. They could have their meal brought in, and he could eat in his cabin alone, with space to think.

SHELLEY TRIED to deal with the idea that she could be falling in love with Lucas while she took a shower and changed into linen slacks and a loose white blouse. By the time she was ready to go up and Lucas came into the cabin, she thought she had control over whatever madness had been infecting her. But the first glimpse of the man shattered that foolish idea.

Even teenage crushes hadn't caused her this much turmoil. He strode into the cabin, control like a mantle around him, but she had to force herself to act casually. She had to force herself not to dwell on the way his hair had been carelessly raked back from his face as if he'd been impatient to get it over with. Or the way he held his left arm close to his side and didn't move it very much.

She remembered the fall to the pavement when he'd pushed her out of the way of the bus, and the idea that he must have hurt himself even more made her feel horribly guilty. But she didn't say anything as they left the cabin with Emily.

On the way up to the display in the playroom, Emily slipped between them as if it was the most natural thing to do. And when they got to the entry of the playroom, a line of parents had formed.

Emily tugged at Shelley. "This is where the parents wait until everything's ready. You two can go inside when they tell you, and I'm suppose to get behind my table for when you get there, then I can show you everything.''

Lucas put a hand on Emily's shoulder. ''Why don't you stay here with us until we get in the room?''

Emily frowned at him. ''But I'm just going to be there.'' She pointed to a table across the room. ''I'll stay right there and you can see me, can't you?''

Shelley could feel the hesitation in her echoed in Lucas, but he finally agreed. ''All right, but don't go anywhere else. Stay right at the table.''

''I will, Lucas,'' she said and smiled at him. ''Thanks.''

''Sure thing,'' he murmured, then she ran into the room.

As Shelley watched Emily rush across the room, she felt a sinking feeling in her stomach. There hadn't been too many men in Shelley's life, and certainly none serious enough for Emily to even begin to think there could be more to it than friendship. The child understood why Lucas was here, she'd explained it to her. But the feeling that Emily was getting involved in some sort of fantasy about this being a romance, worried Shelley. Dreams hurt so much when they shattered. She knew that all too well, and she didn't want Emily to experience it.

She watched Lucas keeping a close eye on Emily, then a lady in a uniform started letting parents into the room. When she got to Shelley and Lucas, she smiled brightly at them, but spoke to Lucas. ''Your child's name, sir?''

''My daughter is Emily Kingston,'' Shelley said quickly.

"She's at table ten. Go on in."

Shelley walked with Lucas into the room that held a huge Christmas tree and long tables filled with bright ornaments and toys. At Emily's table, they found her talking to another little girl. The other child looked up at Shelley and Lucas when Emily said, "Mommy, look." She had a small display of silver balls studded with sparkles, and a plastic doll dressed like an angel. "These are what I made."

"They're beautiful," Shelley said as she lifted one of the balls. "You did these all yourself?"

"They showed us some, then let us do it."

"Didn't Martha help?"

Emily frowned at Shelley. "No, big people weren't supposed to. Besides, Martha had other things to do."

Lucas dropped to his haunches by the table, getting to Emily's eye level. "What things?"

"I don't know. She had to go for a bit."

"She left you here alone?"

"I'm seven. I don't need a baby-sitter. Besides, she told me to stay here and she'd be back. I wasn't supposed to leave the room, and I didn't."

"You did the right thing. That's very smart of you. But do you know where Martha went?"

Emily shrugged, obviously bored with the subject. "Nope." She reached for the angel and held it up to Lucas. "Do you like this?"

"Sure do." He straightened up and touched the angel's pipe-cleaner halo.

"Can you tell it's an angel?"

"Of course I can. Does she have a name?"

Shelley could see Emily considering the question, then she said, "Her name's Ashley."

"Ashley, that's a nice name."

"I always wanted to be called Ashley. It's such a pretty name, don't you think?"

"Emily's pretty nice, too," Lucas said.

She wrinkled her nose with mild distaste. "It's simple and old-fashioned."

"Where did you hear that?" Shelley asked, never suspecting that Emily had thought about a new name.

"Miss Lillian. She said Emily is like Lillian and Jessica, simple and old-fashioned. But Ashley's a real pretty name."

"When were you talking to Lillian?" Lucas asked.

"I saw her and Jessie when Martha and me were coming to the cabin. Miss Lillian and Miss Jessie said that they wanted me to sit between them at the table at dinner tonight. They seem real nice, don't they?"

"Yes, they do," Shelley said.

"I thought we could have dinner in our cabins," Lucas said abruptly.

Emily looked at Lucas. "How come?"

He seemed taken aback that she questioned his idea. "We've had a long day, and I thought—"

"But they're going to light up the Christmas tree. Miss Lillian said that I can't miss it." She shifted to Shelley. "I have to be there, Mommy. I need to do something real important tonight."

Shelley looked at Lucas without saying a word. This was up to him completely.

When Lucas frowned at her, Emily piped up with, "Are you mad again?"

He seemed taken aback, but muttered, "I'm always mad about something."

"That's too bad," Emily said with great seriousness. "Maybe it's because you don't have any kids. If you had kids you'd have more things to worry about than yourself."

"Oh, really?"

"Sure, that's what Miss Jessie said. She never had kids, but she was a schoolteacher. She says that it was like her having thousands of kids. When you have kids around, you don't have time to think about yourself. But you don't have any at all, and you need some, just one or two maybe."

Shelley felt her heart sink. She'd been right to worry about Emily beginning to think about things that could never be. She couldn't even look at Lucas. "Emily, that's not polite to say things like that."

"I'm sorry." She held the angel out to Lucas. "Here. You have Ashley and she'll make you happy."

He didn't reach for it. "You keep Ashley for your own Christmas tree."

"We only have little Christmas trees. Ashley would be way too big for it, and you need her more than I do."

Lucas took the angel, dwarfing it in his hands. "Are you sure?"

"I sure am," she said with a smile. Then she looked at her mother. "Can we go and get ready for dinner now?"

"Sure, let's go," she said.

Without a word, Lucas went with Shelley and Emily out onto the deck, and he stayed silent until they were at the door to their cabin. He turned to Shelley with the silver angel in his hand. "At dinner we'll just stay long enough to eat, then come right back down here."

She frowned at him. "Is there any special reason for that?"

His expression tightened. "That's the way it needs to be," he murmured, then glanced at Emily, a slight smile barely touching his mouth. "You're quite an artist."

"You like Ashley?"

"She's very pretty. You did a good job on her."

Emily actually blushed. "Thanks."

He watched while Shelley opened the door, then he glanced inside to check the room, then motioned them to go in. But instead of following them, he stood in the hallway. "We'll go up at seven for the meal."

"Fine," Shelley said, facing him, feeling as awkward as a teenager. "Seven it is."

He reached out and for a moment she thought he was going to touch her, but his hand went past her arm to grip the door handle. "Lock this door," he said, then pulled the door shut without coming in.

It was the first time he hadn't come in with her, and she could hear him walking away, then his door clicking open, then shut.

"He's still mad, isn't he?" Emily asked softly.

Shelley stared at the connecting door as a thud sounded in the cabin. "He's not mad. He's . . . he's preoccupied."

Emily tugged on Shelley's arm. "He liked Ashley, didn't he?"

Shelley looked at her daughter. "Yes, I believe he did."

"The lady who was helping us make the angels said that angels make people really happy. That angels are good and light and—"

"They're a myth," Shelley said quickly.

Emily started to turn around and around slowly, her arms held out at her sides, her head tipped to look up at the ceiling. "And they can fly way up into heaven."

"Emily?"

The child stilled and looked at her mother. "I know. It's pretend. But I'm using my 'magination. That's how you can fly, if you pretend. And Santa Claus—"

"Is pretend."

"I know, but sometimes I think maybe if a lot of people think it's so, maybe it's not just pretend."

Shelley had no idea why she was suddenly feeling very much like the Grinch who stole Christmas. "You understand the difference between reality and fantasy, don't you?"

"Sure," Emily said as she crossed to the bed and flopped down on the spread. "But sometimes it's sort of nice to think about flying and Santa Claus and things."

"What things?"

"You know." Emily shrugged. "Things."

She moved to the bed and sat by Emily. "Listen, Emily, sometimes we wish things were different, that we had things that others did, but that doesn't make it so."

Emily cast her a narrowed look. "Santa Claus was at the party and he said that if we don't wish for things, we'll never get them."

The child she'd known in San Francisco was changing right in front of her eyes, and it was scaring her. It was one more particle of control she felt slipping away from her as surely as her own emotions were being turned topsy-turvy. "But wishing doesn't make a difference." If wishes could alter life, Lucas wouldn't have pushed her away. "It's work and dedication that make things work out. Like my job, or your schoolwork. Not wishing on a star or making believe that things are different than they are."

She could tell Emily was thinking about that, then she looked up and nodded solemnly. "Yeah, that's it."

"What is?"

Emily got up and started for the bathroom. "Can I wear my pink dress tonight?"

"Sure. What's *it?*" she asked.

As Emily got to the bathroom door, she looked at Shelley and her expression was uncharacteristically guarded. "I figured it all out."

Shelley stood. "Figured out what, Emily?"

"How to do things," she said, then went inside and closed the door.

LUCAS PUT THE ANGEL on the nightstand and reached for the red ball. As he gripped and regripped the rubber, he paced the cabin. He should have let Shelley go home. He should have told her that the ship was a bad idea. But the cop in him knew it wasn't, that it was the best way to protect her in a limited area . . . if there really was someone after her on board.

He paused by the nightstand and looked down at the angel. Life had grown so complicated in the past few days. And Lucas felt as if he'd been pulled into a vortex of confusion that refused to let him go. He gripped the ball so tightly that his arm felt as if it were on fire, and he had to ease his fingers.

Since he'd hit the pavement with Shelley in his arms, his shoulder had been hurting like crazy. He turned and went into the bathroom and picked up the small bottle of painkillers. He stared at the bottle for a long moment, then put it down. He couldn't afford to have his thinking fuzzy or his reactions dulled. It had been too close in Ensenada.

He reached into the shower stall, turned on the water full blast and stripped off his clothes. When he stepped under the hot jets of water, he stood very still and let it beat against his scarred shoulder until the skin began to tingle. After what could have been a moment or an hour, he felt some tension easing in him.

He reached for a towel, then stepped out onto the coolness of the floor. As he turned off the water, the silence beat on his ears, then he heard something in the next cabin. Movement, soft thudding sounds, then Emily laughed and Shelley joined in with her daughter.

Lucas began to scrub his skin with the terry-cloth towel, hating the way just a sound could make him feel as if he was on the outside looking into a place that held warmth and joy . . . and Shelley.

Chapter Eleven

The tree in the main ballroom was laden with crystal ornaments and tinsel. It was another version of the one in the dining room, but this *was* a Christmas cruise, Lucas thought. As he walked into the main room with Shelley and Emily just after seven, a string quartet was playing "Silver Bells," and most of the diners were already seated at their assigned tables.

Lucas let Emily walk between him and Shelley, staying close but not too close and not kidding himself that he belonged with them. If there wasn't a case he was working on, Shelley would have never collided with him. She wouldn't even have come close.

He purposely didn't look directly at her. He didn't have to see her hair caught up in a riot of curls by silver clips, or the way a simple lavender dress in some sort of silky material clung to her slender body. He couldn't, and he wouldn't, let that image assault his senses. That's just what it was. An assault, and he had to stop it in its tracks.

When they got to their assigned table, Lucas was about to maneuver Emily to sit between him and Shelley, but Jessie didn't give him a chance.

"Wonderful that you came," Jessie said with a large smile, and patted the empty chair between herself and Lillian. "Sit with us, Emily, if it's all right with your mother?"

"It's fine with me," Shelley said as she took her seat, and Lucas had no alternative but to sit right beside her.

Major mistake, he thought as he inhaled the delicate scent that she wore and sensed her heat at his side.

To distract himself, he glanced at the other diners. James Sloan was at the end of the table nursing a drink, his face flushed and his eyes on Shelley. The newlyweds were whispering to each other as if the rest of the table was empty, and Brant Weston sat back in his chair looking striking in a white dinner jacket and dark, tieless shirt.

"Are you recovering after your little bit of excitement in Ensenada?" Brant asked Shelley, and Lucas suddenly remembered seeing Brant near the bus accident.

"You were there, weren't you?" Lucas asked.

Brant fingered a wine goblet that looked as if he hadn't touched the liquid in it at all. "Yeah, and I saw the whole thing. Damn lucky that Shelley wasn't hurt."

"Very lucky," Lucas murmured.

"Absolutely," Jessie echoed. "Very lucky." She shivered. "That bus, my goodness, it was so close to Lucas and Shelley. Thank God, it didn't hit either one of them."

"A bus?" Emily asked, looking up from picking at a Jell-O salad done in green and red with ribbons of white through it. The pink dress she was wearing put color in her cheeks, and her blond hair was pulled back in two braids. "You didn't tell me about a bus," she said to Shelley.

"What in the hell are you all talking about?" Sloan asked with a touch of belligerence.

"Shelley tripped and almost fell in front of a bus. Lucas managed to get her out of the way," the professor said. "Very fast thinking, indeed."

Emily turned to Lucas, her eyes enormous. He'd thought she'd be terrified at the thought of her mother almost getting killed, but that was being overridden by some inner excitement. "Wow, you didn't tell me that you saved my mom's life!"

He wasn't at all comfortable being put up as a hero, especially with this child. "I just helped out."

"Did he really save my mom's life?" she asked Lillian.

"Yes, he did. Lucas didn't think twice. He got your mother to safety in the nick of time."

Emily clasped her hands together. "That's great!"

"It was frightening," Shelley said.

"I just did what anyone would have done," Lucas said.

"Like hell you did," Sloan muttered. "I wouldn't have hit the pavement for a lawyer. What's the old joke, what do you call ten dead lawyers at the bottom of the ocean? A good start." He laughed thickly at his own joke and seemed oblivious to the others at the table. "A *very* good start."

"My good man, that is no way to talk in front of the lady or her daughter," the professor said.

Sloan shook his head. "That's no lady, that's a lawyer."

Lucas looked at Sloan. "That's enough. You're way out of line."

"What are you going to do, challenge me to a duel of honor? Just because she's a looker, you're willing to ignore what she does?"

Lucas spoke before he really thought. "She's just doing her job, a job someone has to do, and she's damned good at it." As the words came out, he could feel Shelley looking at him, probably with the same shock he was feeling hearing himself defending her career. But he meant every word of it. "So keep your comments to yourself and let the rest of us enjoy our meal."

"Here, here," the professor said.

Sloan glared at Lucas. "Where do you get off shoving people around and acting as if you're interested in the lady's mind, when we all know what you're after?"

Lucas clenched his hands into fists, and that sent pain radiating through his left arm and shoulder. "Sloan, shut up before you go too far."

"Isn't that where you're planning on going?" Sloan jeered.

Lucas got to his feet so quickly that his chair almost toppled backward. "That's it. You're asking for it. We've had more than enough of your drunken insults."

"Lucas isn't going anywhere, Mr. Sloan," Emily said in a voice that carried. "And you leave my mommy alone. You've got a bad attitude."

Lucas watched Sloan's face turn deep red as he looked around the table, then he glared at Lucas. "Drop dead, Jordon," he muttered, then got up, said something about "the brats of this world" and staggered off.

Brant Weston had sat silently during the verbal combat, but as Sloan left, he said, "What's he talking about that you shove people around?"

Lucas sank down in his chair, watching Sloan veering off by the door to go into the piano bar. "Sloan was drunk last night and got out of line with Shelley. Just let it rest that he ended up on his back on the deck."

"You punched Mr. Sloan?" Emily asked in a voice that told Lucas the hero thing was starting up again. And it made him even more uncomfortable, especially after Sloan's crude accusations.

"No, Emily, I just pushed him. It wasn't anything."

Brant studied Lucas. "It sounds suspiciously as if you've appointed yourself Shelley's bodyguard."

Shelley watched Lucas stare at Brant for a long, hard moment, then he suddenly smiled, a jarringly out-of-context expression. "Sure, a bodyguard with a bum arm and hand? I don't think so. I'm just good at bluffing around guys like that and tripping them when they aren't looking."

"At least he got Sloan to go away," Jessie said. "I know the man's had a hard time and it is Christmas, but one shouldn't be expected to put up with that." She looked at Lucas. "And if you pushed him onto the deck last night, I'm quite sure he deserved it."

As the waiters began to serve the meal, the newlyweds got up and without a word walked away practically wound around each other. Shelley hadn't learned much about them, but she found herself almost envying them. Everything was so simple for them. Being in love. It seemed that anytime she even entertained the idea of love, it blew up in her face.

"Shelley?"

She turned to Jessie. "I'm sorry. What did you say?"

"We're going to the Christmas concert after dinner, would you like to come?"

Lucas spoke up before Shelley could. "Shelley was just saying on the way here how tired she was...especially after everything that's happened."

"Yes, I am tired," she said with real truthfulness. "I think I should take it easy tonight."

"Mommy, there he is," Emily said, and Shelley looked up to see Santa Claus approaching their table with a hearty, "Ho, ho, ho. Merry Christmas to all of you."

His portly stomach shook with each laugh, and Shelley had to admit that from the plush, fur-trimmed red suit to what appeared to be a real beard, the man looked the part.

Emily waved at him, and he circled the table to where she was sitting. "Well, Emily. How nice to see you again." He looked at the table at large. "This little lady made a very special angel today."

"I named her Ashley," Emily said.

Santa laughed. "That's a nice name for an angel," he said, his hands on his ample stomach as he bent toward her.

"I gave her to Lucas. He doesn't have any kids and I wanted him to be happy."

"That's a very nice idea, Emily, and very kind of you."

"I decided what I wanted."

Shelley watched Emily, and knew she was caught up in the magic of Christmas. She just hoped that it wouldn't hurt too badly when it began to fade.

"Well, since you've been a very good girl this year, helping your mother and doing well in school, I don't see why you can't get what you want for Christmas. Now..." He leaned closer to her. "Tell me what it is that Santa can bring you this year."

Emily looked at Shelley, then up at Santa and motioned him to come closer. She whispered something in his ear, and as Santa straightened, he stroked his long white beard. "Now, that's a tough one."

Emily seemed to sink in her chair, the glow fading rapidly from her face, and it broke Shelley's heart. "I know. You can't do it," Emily said. "But that's okay. I didn't think—"

"Emily," Shelley said quickly. "You can't expect things to happen—"

Santa held up one white-gloved hand. "Oh, no, I didn't say I couldn't do it. I just said it wouldn't be easy." He looked at Emily. "I'll do the best I can, I promise you that. It's Christmas, Emily. Anything's possible." Then he took a candy cane out of his pocket and gave it to her. "Merry Christmas to you," he said with a wink, then looked around the table. "Merry Christmas one and all."

Shelley didn't know if she was angry at the man playing Santa for setting up hopes in Emily that probably would be dashed, or if she should find out what it was Emily wanted and make sure she got it. As Santa walked to the next table, Shelley asked, "So, what did you ask him for?"

"That's a secret," Emily said.

"Then how are we going to know if you get it or not?" Lillian asked.

"I'll tell you," she said.

"I wish Santa had asked me what I want for Christmas," Brant murmured as he looked at Shelley.

She could feel her skin crawl at the way he let his gaze glide over her, and she reached for her fork.

But he didn't let her off the hook. "How about another dance? Our last one was interrupted."

Shelley shook her head. "I'm starved. All I want to do is eat right now."

Brant frowned at her, obviously used to getting his way with women. "After you finish dinner?"

She began to prod at her chicken with her fork, and didn't meet his gaze. "I'm tired and sore. Thanks, anyway."

"You're lucky you're in one piece," he muttered, then stood and tossed his napkin on his untouched meal. "I'll be around later. Maybe you'll change your mind. Meanwhile, I think Sloan's got the right idea. A drink sounds pretty good."

With a general nod to the table, he headed off in the direction of the piano bar. Shelley cast Lucas a slanted glance, but he was watching Brant leave. Then he suddenly turned to her, his dark eyes unreadable. "He's got a real problem," he said.

She shrugged. "Yes, he does."

The professor offered his opinion. "You know, I saw him in town today, right by the curb before you fell, then he just disappeared. You would have thought he'd stay to make sure you were all right. But I bet he took the launch that left just before we got to the landing."

Shelley was getting more and more edgy. She knew someone had touched her back, that there had been strength pushing her forward. Slowly, she looked around the table at the remaining people, people who looked completely normal and innocent. Yet did she really know anything about them? The sisters, the professor, Brant, Sloan, even the newlyweds?

She didn't have any idea who was who anymore. She barely recognized herself, she barely recognized Emily, and she wanted nothing more than to get to the safety of her cabin and bolt the door, locking her and Emily inside.

She pushed away her half-eaten dinner, her appetite completely gone, and she looked from the table to the Santa who was making his way around the room. Brant and Sloan were nowhere in sight, and the newlyweds were sitting on stools against a brass rail near the Christmas tree. They were watching the room, and for the first time since she'd met them, they weren't touching.

When Lucas tapped her hand where it rested on the table, her usual reaction, to jerk away from contact with him, never materialized. As she looked at him, she knew that he was the only one she fully trusted on this ship, the one person who seemed like an island of sanity in a sea of insanity, a man she could love. Love? Trust? When was the last time those two emotions had been part of any relationship she'd had?

"We should be getting back to the cabins," he said.

She nodded and started to stand, but Lillian stopped her. "Shelley, since you're too tired to go to the Christmas show, would it be all right with you if we took Emily?" She glanced at her watch. "The show starts in half an hour, and I think it's an hour long." She looked at Shelley. "We can bring her back to your cabin by ten."

Lucas was still touching her hand, and she didn't miss his discreet pressure. "I appreciate the offer, but I think Emily and I are going to spend some time together tonight."

"But, Mommy, I—"

She stopped Emily's words with a look, tired of fighting her every step of the way. "Not tonight, sweetheart. I'm sure they'll have the show tomorrow night. Maybe we can go then."

The child gave up, but Shelley could see the mutinous look in her eyes. "Yes, tomorrow evening, Christmas Eve, maybe then," Lillian said.

When Lucas stood, Shelley got up and said, "Yes, we can all go."

"That would be quite lovely," Jessie said.

Emily surprised Shelley when she stood and gave each sister a kiss on the cheek as she said good-night. The child didn't have any relatives to speak of, and it was out of character for her to attach herself to strangers so quickly. "Good night, everyone," she said with a smile and a wave of her tiny hand, then she left with Lucas and Shelley.

As they stepped out of the crowded room, Shelley felt Emily take her hand. She'd been doing that lately when she'd been upset, but now Emily wasn't upset at all. When Shelley looked at her, she was shocked to see that she'd slipped her other hand into Lucas's. The man was staring at her, but he didn't draw back.

Emily looked at the sky and said, "Wouldn't it be terrific if it snowed for Christmas?"

Lucas laughed at that, and the easing in his face made Shelley's breath catch in her chest. "If that's what you asked Santa for, you're way out of luck."

"Oh, no, I didn't ask for that."

Shelley took a breath. "You know that whatever you told the old gentleman, he was really being polite and playing a part, don't you?"

Emily looked at her, and the smile on her face was almost smug. "Sure."

But Shelley wasn't reassured at all. "Emily, this whole thing, the Christmas things all around, the way people think, it's all make-believe, all wishful thinking, but that doesn't mean that it changes anything."

"Miss Lillian said that the way you feel and the way you think makes you the person you are. And that if you think good and feel good, that nice things happen."

"The power of positive thinking," Lucas said as they approached the elevators and he pushed the down button with his free hand. "I think there have been a few books written on the subject by very respectable people."

"What kind of thinking?" Emily asked.

"Positive thinking," Lucas said. "Some people believe that if you think about the way you want things to be, that if you believe in those thoughts, it can change the way things really are."

Emily kept holding his hand as she asked Shelley, "Is that true?"

"Emily, people believe a lot of things that aren't true."

"I know. Like the Easter bunny and the tooth fairy. But if you can think things and make them happen—"

"Emily, I can wish I was the Queen of England, but wishing so doesn't make it so. You know that."

"Sure, but—"

Lucas cut in. "Personally, I've always wanted to be Dirty Harry."

That caught Emily's attention, and she twisted to look at Lucas as the elevator doors slid open. "Who?"

"Dirty Harry," he said as they stepped into the car. "You know, the cop in the movies who always knows right from wrong and does it no matter what."

"Why'd they call him dirty? Didn't he take baths?"

"I think he showered regularly, but he did things without worrying about legal loopholes and whether it was by the book. All he wanted to do was to clean up the streets."

As the elevator doors slid shut and the car started down, Shelley watched Lucas, waiting for a zinger about her job from him. But none came.

"Then they should have called him Clean Harry, don't you think?" Emily asked.

Lucas looked taken aback for a moment, then he broke into a true laugh. His face lit up, and he looked years younger, almost boyish.

"I think you've got a point," he said as the elevator stopped. "But my point is, I'm not Dirty Harry, I never will be and I never could be no matter how much I want to be. I'm just a cop. Period."

"But you're brave and strong," Emily said seriously.

As they stepped out of the elevator and started down the corridor, Lucas said, "I'm a cop who's scared all the time. Who worries about if I'm making a difference." He flicked a glance at Shelley. "I think that's what we all worry about."

The connection was sudden and unexpected. To make a difference. That's exactly what she wanted to do, and she knew that Lucas felt the same way. In that moment she understood a great deal about the man. And it only made her turmoil of feelings more confused. Why did he have to be so damned human and so appealing?

Emily let go of the two of them, and turned to walk backward down the corridor so she could look at both of them. "You know, this is all really weird."

"How so?" Lucas asked.

"Mommy and me went to the mountains one Christmas and it snowed. I remember it was so cold and wet, and we went home because I got a bad cold. But this here is like a real Christmas. But it's on a boat, and it's warm and like summer. It's weird.''

They stopped at the door to Shelley's cabin, and Lucas dropped to his haunches in front of Emily. The man seemed to instinctively know that it was good to be on eye level with a child. ''You know what? The best Christmas I ever had when I was a kid was when my brothers and I were all sick with the chicken pox, and instead of presents, my mom and dad gave us all IOUs.''

''What for?'' Emily asked with a frown.

''For Christmas. They said that they would give us a Christmas when we were all well. And we had Christmas two weeks later. It was great because we were all better by then and could have fun.''

''You've got brothers?''

''Three of them.''

''Wow, I wish I had some brothers or sisters. Other kids say that they hate their brothers and sisters, but I wouldn't hate mine. It'd be so neat.''

Shelley stared at her daughter. That was one more thing she'd never known Emily thought about. The closest person in the world to her, and she had a side that she'd never even glimpsed. Or maybe she'd just never looked at it too closely.

''Emily, you didn't ask Santa for—'' she started to ask.

Emily eyed her with a look that said, ''You're hopeless.'' ''Of course not, Mommy. That'd be dumb.''

''I just wondered.''

Lucas straightened and held out his hand for her key. "I think we need to get inside."

She handed the key to him, and as he opened the door, Shelley watched Emily watch Lucas. The child's expression was unreadable, and that made her even more uneasy.

Lucas turned on the lights, checked the room, then motioned them inside. Once inside, Lucas shut the door and locked it, and as he turned, Emily asked, "How come you aren't going to be with your brothers at Christmas, Lucas?"

He shrugged. "The job. It's been a long time since I've been home for Christmas."

"You're a work alcoholic, aren't you? Mommy says that's what she is sometimes."

He grinned, and Shelley wished her own wish, that he'd smile all the time. "I think you mean workaholic, and I don't know about your mother, but I'm guilty of it. Even your mother couldn't get me off on that charge."

"I bet she could. She's real good, isn't she?" Emily asked.

Lucas looked at Shelley, the smile gone and his eyes shadowed by the overhead light. "Yes, she is," he murmured, then barely covered a yawn. "Now, I'm tired. I think I'll call it a night."

"Thank you, Lucas," Emily said quite formally.

"For what?"

"For protecting my mommy."

"It's my job," he said and started for the connecting door.

"Lucas?" Shelley said as he reached to grip the door latch.

He cast a look at her over his shoulder. "Yes?"

"Thanks for everything."

He nodded, then opened the door and went into his cabin. As the door shut behind him, Shelley knew that thanks was pretty feeble for what he'd done for her today.

LUCAS HAD THOUGHT that getting away from Shelley and Emily had been smart. He could rest and have space to think without distractions, but he'd been very wrong. Space didn't diminish the woman's impact on him, and now her daughter was beginning to work her way under his skin.

After he got in bed in the darkened cabin, he laid there for a very long time, sleep as elusive as the answers to the riddle about who wanted to harm Shelley. Then, sometime around midnight, he heard the ship's chimes, and the next thing he knew, it was morning.

He never slept like that anymore, blanking out in a blink of an eye and waking hours later. And he hadn't expected to sleep much, not after the battering his shoulder had taken during the day. But when he opened his eyes, he could see the light of dawn working its way between the narrow opening of the drapes on the windows.

And for the first time in what seemed forever, his arm throbbed, but as he gingerly flexed his muscles, he felt twinges. The pain that had been his companion for so long had mellowed into a bearable ache.

He lay there for a few minutes, then did something he hadn't done for a long time. He reached for the phone and put in a call to Denver. When his oldest brother, Mark, answered the phone, he said, "Hey, Mark, what's going on?"

"Lucas, is that you?"

"It's me."

"My God, it's been a while."

Since he'd been in the hospital after the shooting, to be exact. Then all three brothers, Mark, Matthew and Jonas, had called. "Yeah, it has been a while."

"You're okay, aren't you?"

"Sure. In fact, I'm back on the job."

"Good. You need that. So, how's everything going?"

"It's going," he murmured. "I just wanted to wish you a merry Christmas."

"Don't tell me you're working on Christmas. Bonus pay and something to do?"

"You read me too well, Mark."

"I know, Lucas. And, as I've told you forever, you need to get a life."

He closed his eyes. The words, said casually every time they talked, took on new meaning. A life. He really didn't have one, when it came right down to it. "How'd you get so smart?"

"Being the oldest has its rewards. Brilliance is one of them." He hesitated, then asked, "Is something wrong?"

"No, what could be wrong?"

"With you, I never know. The last time you called, you had your shoulder torn up."

"It's nothing like that this time," he said. The only thing torn up was his peace of mind. "I need to get going, but I just wanted to say hello."

"Sure. You wouldn't consider forgetting the job and coming out here for Christmas tomorrow, would you?"

This was one job he couldn't forget, and he knew he'd never forget. "Can't do, but have a good time. And say hello to Matt and Jonas for me."

"Sure. Lucas?"

"Yeah?"

"Take it easy."

"You, too," he said, and put the receiver in place.

As he lay alone in the bed, memories of Christmases past flooded over him, the family, his parents, the trees and presents. And he knew that in the past ten years or so, he'd let that all go. Suddenly he wanted it back. He wanted family around him. He glanced to his right at the angel Emily had made. And a real tree to put Ashley on.

Chapter Twelve

A sharp knock on the door drew him out of his thoughts, and he eased to a sitting position. "Yes?"

"It's me, Emily."

"Just a minute," he called, and hurried out of bed. He grabbed a pair of Levi's, tugged them on, then raked his fingers through his hair. "Come on in," he said as he sank down on the edge of the bed.

The door eased back and Emily peeked into the room. "Lucas, can I go to breakfast with Martha?"

He leaned forward, resting his forearms on his knees. "Is Martha in there?"

"Yes."

"Could you ask her to come in here for a minute? I'd like to talk to her."

"Sure." Emily turned and called out, "Martha, Lucas wants to talk to you."

The woman came through the door dressed in green pants and a red sweater decorated with poinsettias. Lucas motioned for her to close the door behind her.

As she did, she asked, "You wanted to talk to me?"

"Emily said that you left her alone yesterday."

The woman, with her hair combed unflatteringly straight back from her face, crossed her arms over her middle. "I had to go to the bathroom. I asked one of the women there, whom I know very well, to watch her for me."

"That was it?"

"Ten minutes, tops."

"I'd rather you didn't do that again. There was an incident yesterday that might have been an attempt on Shelley's life. We can't take any chances."

"An incident?"

"I'll explain later, but I need you to be very careful. We don't really know what's going on, and Ms. Kingston is really edgy about Emily. Try to reassure her, and don't take any chances at all when you have the child."

"Absolutely," she said.

"I know you aren't being paid for this, but—"

"I know all about what the mother's been doing, but I like the child. It would be horrible if anything happened to Emily. I know that."

"She's the most important thing in Shelley's life," Lucas said.

"Yes, I know. Anything else?"

"No, just don't let her out of your sight."

"Oh, I won't," the woman said. "You have my word." Then she opened the door and went into the other cabin.

Emily looked in at Lucas. "Did you know this is Christmas Eve tonight?"

"Yes, it is."

"Can I go with Martha?"

"What did your mother say?"

"That it's up to you."

"All right. Go ahead, but stay with Martha. Do you understand?"

"I sure do," she said, and looked at the angel. "Ashley sure is pretty."

"Not as pretty as you," he said, a smile coming for the child without any problem.

She could blush just like her mother. "Bye-bye," she said, then was gone, leaving the door ajar.

Lucas heard Shelley and Martha talking, then Emily saying goodbye. The next thing he heard was a door opening and closing. He stood slowly, stretching cautiously to loosen his muscles, then turned when a soft rap sounded on the partially open door.

He turned to see Shelley looking into the room, her hair tumbled around her face, giving her a soft, sensuous look that touched him immediately. The short robe she was wearing showed her bare legs, and he wished he had on more than just Levi's.

"I'm sorry to bother you," she said.

"What's going on?"

"I was going to ask about swimming. I'd like to try another lesson. What do you think?"

"Sure. Get dressed and we'll head on up."

"Thanks," she whispered, then drew back and closed the door firmly behind her.

Lucas went into the bathroom and closed the door. There was no way to stop the awareness of Shelley from making heat build in him. He was beyond fighting his reaction to the woman. He'd just deal with it and get through it.

SHELLEY DRESSED in her bathing suit quickly, all the while trying to forget the sight of Lucas in tight Levi's, his hair mussed from sleep, the slight shadow of beard darkening his jaw. She didn't want to remember the sight of his body, lean and hard, or the sprinkling of hair on his chest.

She put her robe on over her bathing suit, then pulled her hair into a ponytail, and she stared at herself in the mirror over the dresser in the bedroom. Emily wasn't the only person changing in the past couple of days.

The woman in the mirror looked younger, free of makeup, her hair in a girlish ponytail. And she was about to go up to face the water. When a soft knock sounded on the connecting door, she braced herself, then called out, "Come in," without turning from the mirror.

She heard the door open and saw a flash of movement, then Lucas was behind her, his reflection near hers in the mirror. He was in a terry-cloth robe, and she had a sinking feeling that things were going from bad to worse. He was dressed to go swimming.

"Are you ready to go?"

She turned to look at him. "You're going swimming?"

"It sounds like a good idea. Now, let's go. It's getting late."

She was vaguely relieved. If he was swimming while she took lessons, it might not be too embarrassing. But as they started for the cabin door, the phone in his cabin started to ring. "Let me get that," he said. "It might be Bentley. Then we can leave."

She nodded as he turned and hurried into his cabin. At a slower pace, she followed him, and as she stepped into his cabin, she paused. He was sitting on the side of the bed talking. "Sure, that's fine. Read it to me."

Shelley looked around the cabin at the bed with the sheet bunched in the middle of it, and as she took another step inside, she almost stepped on the red ball Lucas used to strengthen his grip. She stooped and picked it up off the carpet, then started to take it over to him when she spotted a piece of paper on the floor by the hall doorway.

As Lucas listened to someone talking on the other end of the phone line, she picked up the paper. It was a single piece of stiff stationery, not folded. When she turned it over, she saw scrawled handwriting that was all too familiar to her. The ball dropped from her other hand, bouncing off her foot, but she didn't notice.

The person who had been sending her the notes in the city was here, close enough to push this under Lucas's door. And this note was for him.

You won't be able to stop her from getting what she deserves the next time. But you can watch while she pays for everything she's done.

Shelley hadn't been aware that she'd said anything, but the next thing she knew Lucas was beside her, taking the note from her. "Where in the hell did you get this from?" he demanded as he read it.

Shelley could barely form the words. "There," she breathed, pointing at the floor inside the door.

Lucas had the door open before she finished saying the single word, and he rushed out into the hallway as the door struck the wall. Then he slowly came inside and closed the door. "It's empty. They're gone."

He looked at the note again. "You recognize the writing, don't you?"

"It's him...or her. The same one." She hugged her arms around herself to try to stop a trembling that seemed to be building from somewhere deep inside. "I knew this could happen. I mean, I've thought about it, but I...I was hoping..."

"I know. So was I," he whispered as he touched her cheek, the connection searing hot on her cold skin. "But I know what's going on."

She looked at him. "Emily, I need to get to her."

Lucas took Shelley by the arm and led her to the bed. As she sank down on the edge, he crouched in front of her. "Listen to me, Emily's okay for now. It's me the person's communicating with. I need to make a call, then we'll figure out how to get off the ship and disappear."

"What?"

"I can't explain it right now, just sit here. Let me put in the call. Okay?"

She closed her eyes for a moment, then nodded. "Just for a minute."

"Good." He stood and went around the bed to the phone, pausing to pick up the ball on the way, then put it in a dish on the nightstand before he picked up the receiver.

She heard him put in a call, then after what seemed forever, he was speaking in a low, harsh voice. "That was a cheap shot, Dick. Why in the hell didn't you tell me what you were up to?"

The anger in his voice almost burned Shelley, and she hugged her arms tightly around herself.

"Like hell you did. You've gone over the line, and we want off the ship right now."

He listened for a long moment, then answered with one word. "No."

She closed her eyes so tightly that color exploded behind her lids.

"All right. I'll ask, but you'd better make good on this."

He slammed down the receiver and came around to Shelley, crouching in front of her again as she opened her eyes. His face was flushed with anger, but his touch on her leg was gentle, almost reassuring.

"It's been a setup."

"What?" She couldn't begin to understand.

"This whole thing, you, me, the whole damned cruise."

She shook her head. "I don't—"

"Listen to me. Bentley staked us out like goats. He thinks that whoever's after you is with the department, and he arranged this cruise, cutting down the attack area. He subtly let it be known where you were going, and he's sitting back waiting for something like this note to happen."

She swallowed bitterness at the back of her throat. "You're serious?"

"Absolutely. He says that he's got us covered, that there's nothing to worry about. He's got people nearby. But he's lied all this time." He shrugged sharply, and she could tell that he felt as violated as she did by the whole thing. "God, who knows what's true anymore."

"He knew all along and let us walk into it, you and me and Emily?"

"Yeah, he did. He's got his reasons. I know that. But I could kill him for doing this." He stood and raked his fingers through his hair. "God, I've been so stupid. I've been out of practice or I would have spotted it long ago."

She looked at him. "What are we going to do?"

"Bentley said he'll get us off tomorrow when we dock in Cabo San Lucas. Until then, we've got two choices. We can barricade ourselves in here, or go out, be careful and be prepared for the next move."

The idea of hiding was infinitely appealing, but she knew that if she did that, the person would just stay out there, waiting for her to leave her cover. Sooner or later, they'd make their move. Hiding would just prolong the agony.

"I can't just hide. I can't have this going on forever. But Emily—"

"We can keep her in the cabin with Martha, and if she's outside, we'll be with her. We can go and get her now, if you want to."

She wanted to hold onto Emily and never let her out of her sight, but she didn't want to scare her, either. "When she gets back from breakfast, we'll talk to her."

"Good call. Now, what do we do?"

She closed her eyes, then stood and looked at Lucas. "My swimming lesson."

"Are you sure?"

"Absolutely."

"But with one change."

"What?"

"I don't think we should be in a crowd. You're not up to it, and it only makes things more confusing. Besides, there's a lot of kids involved at the lessons, and that's a possible danger."

"You're right."

"I'll give you a lesson in one of the smaller pools. Alone."

The idea of being close to Lucas right now was almost irresistible, but the idea of him touching her was another thing. "I don't know—"

"Hey, I taught my two younger brothers to swim. I'm good."

She actually found she could give a semblance of a smile. "I bet you are."

"Damn straight, lady. Ready to go?"

"Sure," she murmured.

"I've been invited for a front-row seat in this little drama, and I intend to be there, but not as a spectator. Now—" he slipped his arm around her shoulder, a comforting action that touched Shelley without any sexual overtones "—the lesson."

As they walked to the door, Shelley asked, "Are you sure you want to try to teach me to swim? I'm like a lead weight in the water."

"The human body is meant to float, so we'll just have to remind your body how to do it."

"My body's definitely forgotten, *if* it ever knew," she said. But one thing it hadn't forgotten was how to react to a lover's touch. Even though his hold on her was meant for support and comfort, it was rapidly changing to much more.

She was almost thankful when he let her go to open the door and leave. She stayed close to him all the way up to the pools and onto the deck where dawn was brushing the sky with pinks and pale lavenders. The air was fresh and gentle with the hint of heat coming with the day. And Lucas kept his distance.

As they passed the pool where the lessons were being taught, she knew Lucas had been right. There was no way she could endanger the children. Goodness knew how her tormentor would try to get to her next, and causing innocent people to be hurt would be something she couldn't live with.

"Here we are," Lucas said as they approached a lap pool at the deserted far end. "And we have it all to ourselves."

Shelley crossed to one of the many deck chairs that rimmed the area and slipped off her robe. As she turned, the sight of Lucas caused her to gasp. He had discarded his robe on a deck chair, and he stood looking at her, his body clearly defined by the morning light.

The combination of strong legs, narrow hips, broad shoulders and dark hair that trailed down his chest over a flat abdomen to the waist of decent but positively seductive black swim trunks was truly breathtaking. He seemed oblivious to her slack-jawed stare. "Ready?" he asked.

She had to force herself not to redefine his question in her own mind. Ready to *swim* was all he meant. He wasn't even hinting at being ready for him, for his impact on her, for the knowledge that this man was someone who could narrow the world to his own presence.

"Ready," she echoed and headed past Lucas to the edge of the pool where steps led into the clear blue water. "Just tell me what to do."

He was there by her, then in one easy, clean motion, he dove into the water. She watched him skim under the surface, then turn and emerge a few feet from the edge of the pool right in front of her.

The water slicked back his hair and spiked his lashes. As he shook his head to clear the water, he looked at her. "Sit on the edge, and when you're ready, get in." The morning light glinted off skin that was sleek with water, and it exposed the scar at the crown of his shoulder. "Get wet, then we'll start."

She sat on the rough edge, then as Lucas waited patiently, she gradually slid down, inch by inch, until she was finally in the warm water up to her breasts. "Now what?" she asked, holding onto the coping for dear life.

"First, you need to let go of the pool. Let your hands rest at your sides."

"I don't—"

"The edge is right there, inches from where you'll be. And so am I. Nothing's going to happen to you. Trust me."

She never looked away from Lucas as she forced herself to let go of the hard cement. "Okay," she said, putting her arms out to her sides.

"Now, you'll have to put your face in the water."

The idea made her panic. "I . . . I don't think so."

"Shelley, if you can't get water on your face, you can't swim. Besides, you did it for the instructor yesterday."

"I had to, but I didn't want to, and when I did, I knew I couldn't do it again."

"It gets easier, I promise."

"I bet you just jumped in when you were a kid and were swimming in a few minutes."

He smiled at that, and something eased in Shelley. "Close. My older brother, Mark, did the dirty deed. He pushed me in, then made me get to the side by myself."

She grimaced at the idea. "That's horrible."

"I survived, and I love to swim."

"It could have terrified you and you never would have been able to get in the water again."

He came closer to her, and his body pushed the water in front of him, rippling against her breasts. "What happened to you? A brother who threw you in or a sister who pulled you under?"

"I don't have any brothers or sisters."

He came even closer, his hands reaching out on either side of her to grip the coping, and she was neatly caged inside. "Then what happened?"

"I just never learned." She swallowed hard at his closeness. "And you know what they say about teaching old dogs new tricks."

He cocked his head to one side, his damp lashes lowering to narrow his eyes. "You're hardly an old dog, and as for new tricks..."

"I just want to be able to swim, that's all."

"That's what we're here for." He pushed himself back from her and held out his hands. "Take my hands and I'll hold you up. We can move around the pool and see just how much we can do without getting your face wet."

Hesitantly she reached out for Lucas, and when his hands closed over hers, she felt her fear beginning to slip away. He moved backward slowly, taking her with him, and before she knew it, she was gliding through the water, her toes barely skimming the bottom. And she never looked away from Lucas.

She'd never felt such trust in anyone before in her life, and she just let it happen. In the weightlessness of the water, she forgot about everything else and let herself drift.

"You're doing great," Lucas said. "See how simple it is? You just have to relax and let it happen."

She smiled at him. "Yes, just let it happen," she murmured.

"You're staying up, and you can't even touch the bottom here. See how easy it is?"

Until he pointed it out, she had no idea they were in deeper water. But he was right, there was nothing solid under her feet. She'd let herself go right into deep water, the way she was about to do with her emotions, and the thought terrified her. She panicked, scrambling to get a better grip on Lucas, and the next thing she knew, she was sinking.

Chlorinated water rushed into her nose and mouth. Two bodies tangled together in the silent weightlessness, fighting, panicking, going deeper and deeper, then she was being dragged upward. Lucas had her by one arm, and they broke the surface with furious splashing.

Shelley gulped in air as they approached the edge of the pool. Lucas held her up with one hand, his other hand swirling in the water to keep the two of them afloat. "That's not the way it's done," Lucas gasped.

She frantically reached for the coping and gripped it tightly. Lucas let her go, and he wiped at his face, brushing away drops of water. "Are you all right?"

"Yes—I think so. I'm sorry. I just panicked. I don't think I'm made for water at all."

He smiled at her suddenly, a brilliant expression that was as stunning as the sun coming out after a thunderstorm. "I don't know about that. You got your face wet."

"Yes, I guess I did. And I swallowed half the pool doing it." She couldn't quite face that smile, and when she looked away, coldness came from nowhere to envelop her. James Sloan was standing on the far side of the pool just staring at the two of them.

When Lucas saw Sloan, he muttered, "What in the hell is he doing here?"

Then Sloan walked around the pool toward them and Lucas reached for the coping by Shelley, coming so close to her that his feet brushed hers as he kept himself afloat. But he never took his eyes off Sloan.

"What's up?" he said as the man got closer.

Shelley looked at Sloan and was surprised that he looked sober, and much older. Deep lines etched his features. His clothes, a dark shirt and slacks, looked as if he'd slept in them. "I've been looking for the two of you." His gaze went directly to Shelley. "You, in particular."

"What do you want?" Lucas asked.

The man stopped above them. "This is hard for me to say, but I just wanted to apologize. I could tell you it was the alcohol talking, but the truth is, I don't know where the alcohol ends and the person inside begins."

Shelley didn't know what to say. "Mr. Sloan—"

"Let me finish," he said, cutting her off abruptly. "Since my life crashed around my ears, I've been hiding in a bottle. When I'm drunk I can say anything I want to say. But that's over. It can't go on. I'm here to apologize for what I've said to you. I'm sorry for it. Very sorry."

Shelley stared at him. The man was painfully human and obviously in a lot of pain. "It's forgotten," she said.

"I appreciate that. Thank you." He looked at Lucas. "Sorry."

Lucas nodded. "Shelley's right. It's over."

"Thank you, both of you." He looked around. "Will you tell Emily how sorry I am?"

"You can tell her when you see her," Shelley said.

"Just tell her for me," he said, then walked away. Shelley watched him go along the deck toward the front of the ship, then she turned to Lucas. He was watching James Sloan, too, but with a hard expression.

"Don't you think he meant that?" she asked.

"Maybe, maybe not."

"I believed him. He's in a lot of pain."

"Maybe that's what he wants you to think, to put you off guard."

"That's pretty cynical."

He looked at her, his dark eyes without humor. "Damn right it is." He moved and with one stroke he was at the pool edge. Then he lifted himself out of the water. For a second he stood there, his water-sleek body gleaming in the rising sun, and Shelley felt an ache deep in her. Then he was crouching, holding out his right hand to her. "Lesson's over for today."

She reached out to him, and with his help, scrambled out of the water onto the deck. Dripping, she turned and reached for one of the towels the crew had set out on tables around the pool. She quickly rubbed at her hair, then dropped the towel in a basket and picked up her robe. As she shrugged into it, she turned to Lucas. Thankfully he had his robe on, his hair faintly spiked from drying it. A towel was draped around his neck and he was holding each end with his hands.

"It was incredible what Sloan said to us," she said.

As they started across the deck, side by side, not touching, he said, "If he really meant it."

She stared straight ahead. "What if he did mean it?"

"Then it's a miracle."

She looked at her bare feet on the deck. Miracles. She would consider meeting someone like Lucas was a bit of a miracle . . . if she believed in them.

Chapter Thirteen

Shelley glanced at Lucas and found him studying her as they walked. Heat touched her face, and she felt that sensation of the world narrowing, the way the rest of the world seemed to slip farther away when he was near. "What was that call about in the cabin before we got the note?" she asked, hoping to divert her thoughts.

"It was someone Bentley had checking on things for me, and they confirmed something Bentley told me about earlier."

She stopped by the railing and stared out across the calm waters of the Pacific. "What things?"

"An update on Brant Weston." He stood by the rail, his arm brushing hers. "The man's got big trouble."

She glanced at Lucas, and he was staring straight ahead, his right hand gripping the rail so tightly his knuckles were white. "What sort of trouble?"

"It seems that an old girlfriend of his is bringing charges against him for sexual assault."

"Oh, my God. Are you serious?"

He cast her a slanted look. "Very serious. When he gets back, he'll be picked up as soon as he sets foot off the ship. If I was him, I'd stay in Mexico."

She looked at the water. "That's horrible. I mean, he makes me uneasy, but I never thought he was that low. He looks so normal."

"I told you before that there isn't any look that a criminal has. There certainly isn't any special look that a rapist has."

"I guess not," she breathed.

"We need to get down to change, then see if we can get some breakfast."

"What about that caroling thing tonight?"

"We'll play that by ear." He tapped her shoulder. "And tomorrow when we have our lesson, we'll learn how to go under the water when we *want* to go under the water."

"Good," she said. "I'll be looking forward to it."

"So will I," he murmured, his voice creating a knot in her stomach, but when he touched her shoulder, the contact was impersonal. "Now, let's go and get breakfast."

THE DAY SLIPPED PAST with surprising speed for Shelley, and nothing out of the ordinary occurred. She didn't let Emily out of her sight, and Lucas stayed right with her and Emily while they went through the ship's shops and had lunch with the professor and the sisters. Sloan was nowhere to be seen. Brant Weston never showed, and the newlyweds were always there, but absorbed in themselves.

By the time the three of them headed down to the cabin after dinner, they'd decided to go to the Christmas show together. Shelley decided to change out of her black velvet dress, and Lucas had mentioned something about leaving his tweed jacket behind and going up in his shirt and slacks.

During it all, Shelley had almost managed to put the note and Bentley's deception out of her mind. Tomorrow they'd get off the ship in Cabo San Lucas, fly home and face what had to be done then.

But when they walked into her cabin, the phone in Lucas's cabin was ringing. Lucas bolted the door, then left her and Emily in their cabin while he went to answer the phone.

"This is so neat," Emily was saying while Shelley was trying to hear the conversation in Lucas's cabin. "Don't you think so?"

Shelley asked, "Think what, sweetheart?" her attention on the muffled voice beyond the walls.

"This whole thing, Christmas and stuff. Santa knew my name and he's going to get me a real special present."

That caught Shelley's full attention, and she turned to look at Emily who was busy rummaging through the dresser drawers. "Didn't I bring something red to wear?"

"I don't know." She crossed to Emily. "Sweetheart, what special present?"

Emily stopped her rummaging and looked at Shelley. "You'll find out."

She couldn't deal with this right now. "Emily, the man playing Santa was being nice. He's polite and kind."

"Mommy, I know, I know. It's the spirit of Christmas that's special. I know that."

"Where did you hear that?"

"From the professor. He says that it's the spirit that makes people change and be nice. Like what you said about Mr. Sloan. He's all changed. You said that he was real nice to you and Lucas."

"Yes, he was, but—"

"It's the spirit." She turned and reached into the mess of clothes to pull out a red sweater with green stars embroidered on it in sparkly yarn. "This is great. Miss Lillian said that I should wear something red to the Christmas show."

Lucas came in the room, and when Shelley turned to him, she could tell something was wrong. "Emily, go and change if you want to wear that sweater."

The child went into the bathroom, and once the door was closed, Shelley crossed to Lucas. "What is it?"

He glanced at the closed bathroom door, then leaned closer to Shelley. "It's James Sloan. He tried to kill himself."

Shelley pressed a hand to her chest. "How?" she breathed.

"Pills and alcohol. He left a note about life being worthless. That he wasn't living, just taking up space." Lucas raked his hand through his hair and exhaled harshly. "He almost did it. But a purser had to go to his cabin for something and found him in time. He's in the dispensary, and they're keeping it as quiet as possible."

"Oh, how can I tell Emily?"

"You don't have to right now. Later, or not at all. She doesn't need to know."

When a knock came on the cabin door, Shelley found she couldn't move to answer it. Lucas took one look at her and understood. He touched her shoulder, then went past her to the door. "Martha," he said, and Shelley turned to see the woman coming into the room.

She was all in red, from stretch pants to an overblouse and a clip with a poinsettia on it in her hair. "Hello, there. Did you two hear about that Mr. Sloan?"

Shelley lifted a finger to her lips. "Shh. I don't want Emily to know just yet."

"Oh, sure. No problem. That's not why I'm here, anyway. I was talking to those two ladies, the Warden sisters, and they said that you were all coming up for the play."

"We were planning on it," Lucas said.

Emily came running out of the bathroom, the sweater on with a black skirt, and she'd tied red ribbons on her braids. "Martha. Are you coming to the play?"

"That's why I'm here. Lillian and Jessie told me you were going, and I thought we could all go together."

"Yeah, that's great." Emily turned to Shelley. "Can we go now?"

Lucas touched Shelley on the arm, but he spoke to Martha and Emily. "You two go on ahead and save us some good seats. I need to talk to Shelley for a minute."

Martha looked at Emily. "Well, what do you say?"

"Sure." She looked at Shelley and Lucas. "You two hurry up or you'll miss the three wise men."

"We'll be there soon," Shelley said.

"Stay right with her," Lucas said to Martha.

The woman nodded, then took Emily by the hand and left. When the door closed behind them, Shelley turned to Lucas. "You shouldn't have let them go like that, not now. Why did you do that?"

"I thought you might need a few minutes to get yourself together after finding out about Sloan."

That touched her. It had been a very long time since someone had worried about her or taken care of her. And right now, she liked it. "Thank you. I really could use a few minutes."

"I've got a bar in my cabin. Let's get a drink while you catch your breath, then we'll get up there to see the play."

She went with him into his cabin, and it was only lit by a small light near the phone. He motioned her to two chairs placed to face the view out his window. "Sit and relax," he said as he opened the drapes to expose the night.

She dropped down in the softness of the upholstered chair and looked out at the view as Lucas said, "I'll get us something." He moved past her. "Brandy okay?" he asked from behind her.

"Fine," she said and heard the clink of glass against glass as the faint strains of Christmas carols filtered in from far off. She took off her black pumps as she watched lights twinkling way off on the mainland, and the velvet blackness of the night sky, dotted with stars and a sliver of a moon.

Lucas came to offer her a glass, then she took the cool crystal and kept her eyes on the night. "It's incredibly sad to think of someone being in so much pain that they don't want to live."

Lucas shrugged out of his jacket, laid it on the dresser, then settled in a nearby chair. "It's sad, but the truth is, life hurts. I think that's an unwritten rule. You've seen that. I sure as hell have."

"Maybe we see it all too much," she murmured and took a sip of the smooth liquor.

"Personally or professionally?" he asked.

She closed her eyes for a moment as the brandy spread warmth in her middle, then opened her eyes to the night. "Both, I guess."

"It's been hard for you bringing up Emily alone, hasn't it?"

"Sometimes. But the good outweighs the bad." She fingered her glass. "How about you? What's the best thing in your life?"

"You forget, your daughter told you I'm a work alcoholic."

She chuckled softly, surprised at how comfortable it was sitting here in the semidarkness with Lucas just talking without any of the sharp barbs that had stood between them since they met. "Oh, yes, Emily has a way with words, doesn't she?"

"Tell me something?"

"If I can."

"What do you think of me?"

She shifted in the chair to look at him. The night touched him, pulling him into the shadows, but she could see the look on his face. He was serious about the question. "You? You're a protector of people, a man who doesn't like to give pain. I think you're honorable and loyal and you think that anyone who messes with your version of the law should be shot at dawn."

That brought a rough burst of laughter. Then she saw him toss the last of his drink to the back of his throat and put the glass on the table that sat between their chairs. "Shot at dawn?" he murmured in a low voice. "I hardly think that's the fate I'd prescribe for you."

The mood was shifting so radically that Shelley could barely breathe. And she knew she had to ask Lucas, "What would you prescribe for me?"

He was very still, his eyes never leaving her face, then she heard him take a deep breath. "You don't want to know."

"Yes, I do," she said and knew it was very important to her to hear him say exactly what he thought of her. "What do you think of me?"

He studied her intently, then spoke in a low voice. "You're beautiful, intelligent, and I never thought I'd say this a few days ago, but you're obviously one hell of an attorney."

"Should I be shot at dawn?" she whispered.

He stood abruptly and went to the window, keeping his back to her. "No." The single word was said so softly she almost didn't hear it.

She put her glass by his, then got up and crossed to where he stood. "What do you want to do with me?"

He kept his back to her. "That's a leading question, counselor."

"I know," she whispered, a need for this man growing in her with an intensity that was shaking her to her soul. But she wasn't going to turn back or hide. She knew she couldn't anymore, that she had to stop running where this man was concerned. If he didn't want her, she had to know. If he did, she needed to know that, too.

She touched his back with the tips of her fingers and felt his sharp intake of air. "Lucas?"

He turned slowly to face her. As she looked at him, he framed her face with the heat of his hands, the contact as unsteady as the beat of her heart was right then. His thumbs moved slowly on her cheeks, their caress sending shock waves through her, and his voice was low and rough as he uttered, "I want to make love to you."

Lucas felt Shelley tremble at his words, and he knew the absolute truth in what he said. He wanted to love her in a way no other man ever had or could. And he wanted to know her completely and honestly.

Her tongue touched her lips, and she whispered, "Please, make love to me."

He knew this had never been in the plans, that his life had been a single one for so long that he was hardly fit to draw someone else into it. But there was no strength in him to just walk away from what she was offering him. When her hands spread on his chest, when he felt her touch scorching him through the thin material of his shirt, he knew he was past the point of turning back.

He took her mouth, invading her warmth and tasting her, drawing her breath into his body, and in one stunning moment, he knew that he wanted this woman to be part of him, to be fused in his soul. She circled his neck with her arms, straining toward him, and he could feel every soft curve and angle of her body against him. And his desire exploded, turning from want and need to a fiery ache that threatened to consume him.

With unsteady hands, he fumbled with the zipper on her dress, needing to feel her without the constraints of the velvet between them. As he tugged the zipper down, she moved back, her fingers fumbling with the buttons on his shirt. He slipped the straps of her dress over her shoulders, and they moved apart just long enough for her dress to fall around her feet.

For a heartbeat he saw her in front of him in a skimpy teddy of black lace, then she came to him, offering her lips, and with a frenzy born out of a need that had been building since they first met, he kissed her, tasting her, his hands exploring her body while his tongue explored her mouth.

She parted his shirt, pressing her palms to his chest over his heart. The deep groan that echoed around him came from him. Touch was everything. Taste was everywhere, and the essence of Shelley seeped into his pores. If he could have, he would have swept her up into his arms and carried her to his bed, but with his bad arm, he knew that was impossible.

So instead he drew back, and without a word took her by her hand, leading her to the bed in the shadows. She went with him without protest, her hair freed of the pins to tumble around her flushed face. Then he skimmed off his shirt, and when he undid the button on his pants that barely contained his desire, her hands covered his.

Never looking away from his gaze, she lowered the zipper and eased his pants down. He quickly stepped out of them, and wasn't prepared for her to reach for him, tugging the cotton of his briefs down to free him. When she touched him and circled him, he couldn't contain a shudder. The feeling was exquisite, beyond words, and what little control he had left was gone.

He pulled her to him, falling into the coolness of the bed with her, shifting until she was lying by him, and he tasted her lips, her throat, then the cleavage at her breasts. Impatient to know even more, he slid the black lace off her breasts, and his lips found her nipples, felt them contract into hard buds of desire, and he heard her whimper with pleasure.

With his bad hand he had trouble trying to get the teddy off, but Shelley didn't let that stop them. She moved just enough to undo snaps at the back, then she slid it down and tossed it into the shadows. She lay in front of him naked, unembarrassed and beautiful. Her breasts were full and tipped with rosy peaks. Her stomach, even though she'd had a child, was smooth and silky, and Lucas knew that he'd never seen anyone so lovely in his entire life.

Other women faded into the region of forgetfulness, pushed away by this woman. He lowered his head and kissed her, the contact almost awkward, the feelings so intense that he was having trouble sorting them out. He'd been with others, more than he wanted to think about, but no one had touched his soul...until Shelley.

Shelley felt Lucas's sleek heat beside her, she saw him studying her, his skin sheened with moisture, and she knew with a certainty that she loved him. She had no idea if he could love her the way she knew she could love him, but she wanted what she could have now. If there was nothing later, so be it, but she couldn't walk away.

She touched the scar on his shoulder, her fingers skimming over the knotted skin, and it shook her to think that he could have been killed before she even knew that Lucas Jordon existed at all. The thought jolted her, and she moved closer, pressing her lips to his chest, feeling his heart thundering in unison with hers.

Even his taste was unique, hot and sleek, and when he cupped her hip with his hand, she shuddered. She trailed her touch along his abdomen, feeling the soft hair, following the line downward until she found his strength. Slowly she circled him, relishing the throbbing heat, and she could feel him shudder. It gave her pleasure to know that he wanted her as much as she wanted him, and when his hand found her center, she gasped with ecstasy.

She arched back, willing access to him, and his hand covered her. He pressed the heel of his palm to her swelling. As he slowly began to rotate his hand against her, she felt shards of ecstasy shoot through her, soaring, taking her over. She moaned when his lips found her breasts, and the throbbing sensations intensified until she thought she would die if she didn't feel him inside her.

"Please, I want you," she gasped, and his hand was gone.

She opened her eyes to find him so close she could feel his breath on her face. "I want you," he whispered. "But this shoulder..."

She smiled at him as she shifted, then she was over him, her legs straddling him, and as his gaze held hers, she slowly eased herself down until he filled her. For a long moment she stayed very still, afraid if she moved it would all be over, her feelings were so intense, so raw.

Lucas reached up and touched her face. "God, you're lovely," he groaned, then slowly began to move his hips.

Shelley felt the instant sensations from the friction, and instinctively she began to rock in time with his movements. She braced herself with her hands flat on the pillow on either side of Lucas, and she arched back, closing her eyes. His hands found her breasts, only intensifying the feelings, then they lowered to her hips, drawing her down, sending him deeper into her.

And when she thought she couldn't bear it anymore, when she thought she might die from the pleasure of what was happening, Lucas lifted his hips to meet her in one powerful thrust, and she shattered into a million fragments of joy. She heard someone cry out. She knew it was her own voice mingling with Lucas's as he called her name over and over again.

Then she slowly eased down until she was lying on him, her head resting on his chest, her breathing ragged and shallow. They lay like that for an eternity before she stirred, the last fragments of the pleasure he'd given her lingering deliciously. When she drew back, he caught her face between his hands and kissed her long and hard, then eased out of her and helped her settle by his side.

She cuddled into his heat, one hand resting on his heart, the other over his thighs, and she felt him stroke her arm. The silence in the room was only broken with an involuntary moan when Lucas touched her tender breasts. Then he circled her with his good arm and rested his cheek against her head.

Lying there with him, she wondered how love could come so quickly and so passionately, a deep love that made her want this man in every corner of her life. That thought was intrusive, but she wouldn't allow it to form all the way. She didn't want anything coming between them, not now. She knew it would soon enough, but not now.

She let herself rest against him and relished the feeling of lying with him. Then she closed her eyes and let herself drift into a soft space where there was only Lucas. Nothing else had room there, and she wouldn't let it try to take up residence there.

He pressed his lips to her bent head, then murmured, "The play."

She'd forgotten about it entirely. "I don't suppose we can miss it, can we?"

His laughter was a pleasant rumble in her ear. "We might have missed it already."

She pushed herself up on one hand to look at him. "You don't think we have, do you?"

He glanced at the bedside clock. They'd been in the room for an hour, but it seemed like a lifetime. He looked at Shelley, and a slow smile teased his lips. "We could get there for the last act, I suppose."

She dipped her head, tasting his lips. "Sure," she murmured, and despite the fulfillment of moments ago, her need for this man exploded into white-hot passion.

When his hands touched her, exploring and teasing her, she knew a pleasure that took her breath away, and when Lucas murmured that he wanted her again, she didn't hesitate. She shifted, felt his hardness against her, testing her, then she slipped down onto him and wondered how it could feel so right this fast.

As they began to move together, her wonder grew. To love a person this completely was new to her, despite her failed marriage. What she felt for Rob hadn't even come close to what she felt for Lucas. And as she rode the wave of pleasures with him, she felt a bond growing between them that defied the reality she knew waited for them.

She rose higher and higher with him until she knew that if she let go, she'd fly away with him. And when Lucas murmured, "Let it happen," she did. And the glory of giving herself completely to him bordered on the miraculous. In that moment when everything came together with a perfection that was stunning, she knew that she had her miracle. She and Lucas soared together, and when she finally began to touch earth again, she laid by his side, no words in her to say what she felt.

Lucas held her close, his fingers twined in her hair, and she felt every breath he took. From a distance she heard a phone ringing, and just when she realized it was ringing in her cabin, it stopped. "My phone," she murmured.

Lucas chuckled. "Good thing they hung up. We need time to come up with a good cover story for not showing up on time."

She snuggled closer, closing her eyes as if she could shut out the world with that simple action. Then the phone rang by the bed, and reality intruded. "I'd better get it," she said. "It's probably Emily or Martha or the sisters trying to track us down."

She reached over Lucas, her breasts grazing his chest in the action, and it made her breath catch for a moment. Then she had the receiver and got up on her knees to answer it.

"Go ahead," Lucas said. "I'll give you privacy to lie to them." And with a quick kiss on her cheek, he slipped out of bed and walked naked to the bathroom.

Just the sight of him made her mouth go dry, and she waited until he went into the bathroom and closed the door before she pressed the cold plastic of the receiver to her ear. "Hello?"

"Shelley Kingston?"

The voice was strange, neither male nor female, just low and husky, and she didn't recognize it at all.

"Yes, this is Shelley."

"I thought of killing you for payment," the voice said.

"What?"

The voice went on as if she hadn't spoken at all. "But that was too cheap. I want you to know what it is to lose the one thing you love more than anything else in this world."

"Who is this?" Shelley managed, wishing she could get Lucas's attention, but the door was firmly shut and she could hear water running.

"You'll find out when we come face-to-face," the voice said.

Shelley spotted the red rubber ball on the bedside table and reached for it. With all her might, she threw it across the room at the bathroom door, making a direct hit with a cracking thud. Then it ricocheted back, hitting a wall on the far side of the room before it stopped on the carpet.

When the door opened and Lucas looked out wearing his robe, Shelley motioned frantically for him to come to the bed.

"Are you still there?" the voice demanded.

"Yes, I'm here."

"When I'm finished, you'll wish you were dead. Maybe you'll be luckier at killing yourself than Sloan was."

Lucas dropped down by her, and Shelley pressed her hand over the receiver. "It's the one who wrote the note."

He moved even closer, tipping the receiver so he could hear along with her. He made a circling motion with his hand to tell her to keep her talking.

"Who is this?"

"Lucas Jordon isn't going to help you," the voice jeered. "No one can. Only you will feel the pain of the loss."

"What loss?" Shelley asked.

The laughter on the other end of the line made her skin crawl. "Just ask yourself what's more important to you than anything else, and you'll have your answer."

Shelley felt sickness rising in her throat, and she could barely say, "No...not Emily."

The laughter came again, evil and maniacal. "Have a merry Christmas."

"No," Shelley sobbed into the phone, but the line clicked and the person was gone.

Chapter Fourteen

Shelley tossed the phone onto the bed and scrambled to her feet. She looked around frantically for her clothes, fear rising in her throat. "Not Emily," she said. "Not Emily."

Lucas jiggled the disconnect button of the phone and while Shelley ran into her room to get some clothes, she heard him talking to the ship's security office. "I have to know where the call came from," he said. "Don't give me that bull. You can trace it. Do it!"

As Shelley ran into his cabin in jeans and a loose sweater, Lucas had the phone caught between his shoulder and ear, listening while he managed to get on his pants and shirt. "I'll call you back in a couple of minutes for the information," he said, then slammed down the phone and quickly put on his running shoes.

Shelley went barefoot toward the hall doorway, and Lucas called to her. "Wait."

She turned. "I can't wait. Emily—"

He reached into the drawer of the nightstand, took out his gun, jammed it in the waistband of his pants, then hurried over to Shelley. "All right, let's find her," he said.

Shelley hurried into the corridor with Lucas and headed for the elevator. She didn't care what she looked like, nor that people were looking at her oddly. All she cared about was Emily, getting to her and hiding her from the maniac who had called.

When the elevator didn't come quickly after Lucas pressed the button, he led the way to the stairs. They ducked into the stairwell and hurried up to the main level where the theater was, and broke out onto the deck, which seemed filled with the distant strains of Christmas music. They hurried through the milling crowds leaving the bar and dining hall.

When they got to the entrance of the theater, Shelley was almost out of breath. But she paused only long enough to open the door, then slip into the darkened auditorium with Lucas. The thick carpet felt soft under her bare feet, and on stage the company was acting out "The Night Before Christmas." As her eyes adjusted, she could see enough to spot the sisters sitting with the professor near the back on the other side. Martha and Emily were nowhere in sight.

Shelley hurried across the back of the theater to the last aisle where Lillian was sitting on the end of the back row. She touched the lady's arm as she crouched by her seat, and Lillian turned to her.

"Where have you been?" Lillian whispered, then got a good look at her and frowned. "My dear, what's happened?"

"There—there's an emergency. I came for Emily."

"Emily? She went to get you."

"When did she leave?"

"About fifteen minutes ago. She left with Martha. Since you hadn't come, they were going down to check and see if everything was okay."

"She isn't at the cabin, and I need to find her," Shelley said. "If you see her and Martha, tell them to go to our cabin and wait for us with the door locked."

"Certainly, but do you need help finding her?"

Shelley loved the elderly lady for not needing explanations but offering whatever she could. "Yes, I do."

"Say no more. We'll come and look for her with you."

"Thank you," she said. When she stood up, Lucas was right there. He followed her out of the theater and reached for her arm to stop her. "What did she say?" he asked.

"Emily left with Martha fifteen minutes ago. They were coming down to get us at the cabin."

The sisters and the professor came out and Lillian spoke for the group. "We're going to where they're caroling to see if Martha took her there. Then we'll go down to the buffet area." She patted Shelley on the shoulder. "Don't worry, dear, we'll find her."

Shelley hated the sting of tears behind her eyes. "Thank you so much for helping."

"Page us if you find her, and we'll do the same," Lillian said, then the three of them hurried off in the direction of the music.

Right then a page came over the PA system. "Lucas Jordon, pick up a house phone. Lucas Jordon."

Lucas looked around, then crossed to a bank of house phones just past the entrance to the theater. The message was from Bentley—to call him right away. As soon as he put in the call, Shelley knew that Bentley answered immediately.

"It's Lucas."

"Yeah, all hell's broken loose, thanks to you. What?"

Shelley could see him tense as he listened to the other man for what seemed an eternity, then he finally said, "Are you absolutely sure?"

"What is it?" Shelley asked, but he didn't answer her.

Lucas said, "I will," then he hung up.

"What?" Shelley asked, her nerves stretched to the limit.

"When I was talking to Bentley's man earlier, I happened to mention what a good job Martha Webb was doing with Emily." He shook his head. "Bentley just found out that Martha Webb is in Vermont with her family for Christmas. She never got on the ship. A friend of hers, Gwen Slater, used to work for this cruise line a few years back. She offered to take over for Martha, and they thought Gwen had contacted Bentley to get the okay.

"The thing is, Martha didn't know that Gwen wanted to get to you. She's been under psychiatric care. It seems Gwen was obsessed with Larry Hall, the cop who was shot by Freddy Monroe. She must have found out you were the one who defended Monroe, and she hated you for it. When she found out some way, probably from Martha, that you were coming on the cruise, she put herself here, too."

Shelley swallowed hard, the ache in her throat threatening to shut off her breathing. "She's got Emily. God, we have to find them."

"I know, and this ship is huge."

"Call security and get some help."

He reached for the phone again and punched in three numbers. "Security," he said, but didn't ask for help. Instead he said, "It's Lucas Jordon again. What did you find?"

He listened, then hung up and looked at Shelley. "They traced the call to the top deck at the back of the ship."

Shelley would have taken off immediately, but Lucas grabbed her arm. He looked at her. "Hey, I'm the one with the gun, and I'm the bodyguard. Let me do my job."

His job. It all came down to that. A cop doing his job. But Emily was her life. That was something he couldn't understand. "Do whatever you want to do, but I'm going to find Emily," she said, and took off running.

Lucas caught up with Shelley at the stairs and followed her to the top deck. Once they were free of the stairwell, they took off in the direction of the back area.

At first it looked deserted to Lucas, then he spotted Gwen Slater with Emily at the farthest end by an open service gate in the side rail. The woman was holding Emily's hand, and the child was standing in the opening, precariously close to the edge. When Shelley would have rushed to Emily, Lucas pulled her back, stopping her about ten feet away from the child and the woman.

"Gwen?" he said, leaving his gun in his waistband and hoping he could talk her out of doing whatever it was she thought she had to do with Emily.

The woman froze, then turned, one hand still holding on to Emily. "So, you both came, and you know who I am."

"We wanted to find you and Emily. The play's almost over, and Lillian and Jessie wanted you two to see the ending."

"How come you're calling her Gwen?" Emily asked.

"That's her real name, Gwen Slater," Lucas said. "And we came to get the two of you. Come on, Gwen, let's go."

She didn't move until Emily tried to get out of her hold, then she jerked the child back. "Oh, no, you don't, kid."

Emily twisted to try to get loose, but the woman's hold on her was uncompromising. The child grimaced and gasped, "You let me go! That hurts." She swung at Gwen's hand.

"Too bad. A lot of things hurt in this life. Don't worry, I'll let you go," Gwen said, never taking her eyes off Shelley. "And your mother's going to watch. I'm going to give her her Christmas present. A present like she gave me a few months ago."

"Mommy," Emily said, her voice whiny. "Tell her to let me go back to the play. I don't like this game anymore. I don't want to do it."

"Stand still, sweetheart," Shelley said in a remarkably calm voice. "Mommy and Gwen need to talk a bit, then we'll go back."

"Don't lie to her. You aren't going anywhere with her. Not ever again." Gwen jerked Emily back, right to the edge of the deck. "Never."

"Mommy!" Emily shrieked.

"Your mommy hurt me pretty bad," Gwen said. "She let an animal loose and that animal killed the only person I ever loved. Now she's going to pay for it."

Lucas touched Shelley on the shoulder, unnerved to find her trembling. Yet she was talking as if she was in full control. "Gwen, I didn't do that on purpose," she said. "I didn't know what Freddy Monroe would do when he was freed. I'm so sorry for it. If I had known, I wouldn't have tried to get him off. I swear to you. It was a horrible, horrible thing, and I know you were hurt badly."

As she spoke, she was inching forward, her words covering her actions, and Lucas took advantage of Gwen's full attention being on Shelley. He eased to one side, getting closer, taking his time, letting Shelley talk while he cut down the distance between himself and the woman.

His options were limited, and he knew that the gun wasn't one of them. If he shot the woman, the child would fall overboard. All he could do was wait for his opening, then rush her and hope to hell that he was fast enough to surprise her and grab Emily.

"Hurt me? You don't know how you hurt me. But you will."

Shelley held up her hands, palms out. "Gwen, please, just listen to me. Emily didn't do anything wrong. It's not her fault. It's all my fault."

"It wasn't Larry's fault, either, but he's dead."

"No, of course it wasn't. But don't hurt Emily. Please let her go."

Gwen shook her head. "Sorry. That just isn't possible." She moved Emily back even farther, and Lucas knew that any moment she was apt to push the child off the ship.

When Emily began to cry softly, Gwen muttered, "Oh, shut up," and as she turned to look at the child, Lucas knew he had the only opening he might ever get. He lunged forward, hitting Gwen squarely in the middle, sending her sprawling onto the deck. As he twisted, he saw Emily flailing her arms as she went backward toward the blackness. In a split second, he jerked sideways and grabbed at her with his right hand.

Thankfully, he managed to grip her by her wrist as she started to fall over, and her weight pulled him with her. He reached out blindly, hit his hand on the metal rail and grabbed it. As he jerked to a stop with Emily still in his grasp, agony shot through him. His right arm and leg were off the deck, and Emily dangled like a doll from his hand.

She swung wildly in the air, screaming in terror, and with each movement she made, pain cut through him like a knife. The fiery agony grew excruciating, but he knew if he let go, they'd both be lost. His injured hand was losing what strength it had, and he could feel his fingers slipping on the metal. Then he felt someone tugging on the back of his shirt, and Shelley was there, gasping, "Don't let go," and she had him by his bad arm.

She pulled as hard as she could, and he barely bit back his screams as the pain grew beyond torment. He bit his lip so hard he could taste the blood on his tongue, then his hand gave out and he lurched downward. Shelley screamed, and for a moment he thought they were all going to plunge into the black waters, then he realized his hand had just slipped lower on the post.

Someone else was there, pulling on him, lifting the three of them to the deck and to safety. Lucas tumbled backward, Emily swung over him, and he was staring up at the dark sky. His left arm was limp at his side, almost numb, and someone was trying to lift him and push him back until he was sitting against the railing.

It vaguely registered that the newlywed husband was the one who had helped pull him up and was securing him against the railing. Gwen Slater was lying on the deck unconscious, about five feet from him, with several people bending over her. But it was Shelley and Emily that drew all his attention.

When he saw Shelley clutching Emily to her and he knew they were both safe, he realized that everything had changed. What he'd thought had been a quirk of fate, a job for him to complete, had been his destiny.

He shifted, ignoring the new pain that threatened to tear apart his shoulder. "Shelley," he managed in a hoarse voice. At first he thought she hadn't heard him, then she turned and he reached out with his good hand to her.

Without a word, she stood. Taking Emily by the hand, she came to Lucas. She dropped down to her knees, and with a sob, she buried her face in his chest. With his good arm, he held onto her so tightly that he shook. Emily sat on his outstretched legs, and in that instant when he looked into the child's tear-stained face and felt Shelley against him, he knew that whatever happened, he wanted them in his life. He loved both of them.

That monumental discovery filled him with the sure knowledge that this was what he'd been looking for his whole life. He just hadn't known it until he'd almost lost it all.

"Lucas," Shelley said, her voice muffled against his chest. "Oh, God, I've never been so scared. You started to slip, and you almost fell with Emily. The two of you..." She trembled violently against him.

"Hey, it's all right. We're here, both of us," he whispered, "and you'll never lose us. Never."

She lifted her face to look at him. "Never?"

He grimaced as Emily got closer and put her arm around his neck, pressing against his sore shoulder. "That's the new rule," he managed through clenched teeth.

"Are you sure you mean that?"

"Absolutely," he said, thankful when Emily leaned back to look right at him.

"I can't change the way things are, my work and everything."

He could see the uncertainty in Shelley's eyes, and he spoke with real conviction. "I don't want you to. I think we're the flip side of each other, the missing parts or something like that. Yin and yang, balances for each other."

Emily looked at Lucas and suddenly she was smiling. "You're a hero, Lucas," she said earnestly.

"Emily, I'm not. I—"

"But you are. You saved me and Mommy, and that means that you have to look after us forever."

He blinked. "What?"

"That's what the professor said. He said that in some places when someone saves your life, he owns you. You own us, Lucas, forever."

He knew Shelley was staring at him. "I don't want to own the two of you."

Her smile died as Emily wiped at her damp face. "You don't want us?"

He looked at her, then at Shelley against his side. And the answer came without any hesitation. "Oh, yes I do. I want both of you, very much."

"You do?"

He nodded. "I sure do. In fact, I think we should all get married and you can be my daughter. How does that sound?"

Emily squealed with delight, as if the terror that had just passed had never been. "Oh, can we?"

"We sure can."

"I can't believe it worked!" she said, bouncing on Lucas's legs, jarring his bad shoulder with each motion.

"What worked?" Shelley asked.

"My wish. My Christmas wish!"

"You didn't—"

"I did. I did. And it worked." She got up and smiled at the two of them. "Santa got you to like Lucas and Lucas to like you and we can all be together! Wait until I tell Miss Lillian and Miss Jessie we're getting married!"

Suddenly the professor and the sisters were there, and although the explanation of what had happened got muddled, they understood Emily, who took great delight in telling them she and Lucas and her mother were going to get married. Lucas just sat there, holding on to Shelley.

Then the newlyweds appeared, but they weren't holding each other now. They looked grim-faced, and the man came to hunker down in front of Lucas and Shelley.

"Are you two okay, now?" he asked.

"Yeah, now we are. You pulled us up, didn't you?"

"I barely got to you. What happened with the lady?" he asked, motioning to Gwen sitting motionless on a bench in handcuffs while two men in ship's security uniforms hovered around her.

The change in the man from fawning lover to cool interrogator was stunning. "Who are you?" Lucas asked.

The man grinned. "We're with the SFPD. I'm Russ Jones, and she's Wendy Delano. We were on the cruise to take care of some other business, and Bentley asked us to keep an eye on the two of you just in case you needed some extra help."

"Bentley's got a lot to answer for," Lucas murmured.

The man frowned. "Well, you take care of yourselves, and we'll take care of the woman for you. We don't have much to do until we dock back in the city. Then we've got a collar to make."

Lucas thought a good guess about the identity of the collar would be Brant Weston, but he didn't ask. He just said, "Thanks."

The man stood. "If you need anything, let us know."

Lucas held tightly to Shelley. "I've got everything I need right here."

The sisters came over as Russ Jones headed to where Gwen was sitting. "Well, it was all pretty awful," Lillian said with a smile. "But it certainly ended well. And if we can help, you just ask."

Lucas looked at Shelley, then to Lillian. All he wanted was to be with Shelley, to tell her everything that was deep inside him, to hold her until all of the horror was gone. "I think we just need to get some rest."

"Of course. Tomorrow, you can tell us all about your plans. And we will be invited to the wedding, won't we? I've never seen one for three people before."

Lucas smiled, an easy expression that felt good. "I wonder if the captain's empowered to perform weddings."

"Oh, I don't know. I'll check for you, and let you know," Lillian said. "If he is, maybe we could have a Christmas wedding."

"Maybe we could," Lucas said, then as the sister wandered off to find the captain, he looked at Shelley and whispered, "I love you," just before his lips found hers.

Epilogue

Christmas Day

The cabin was shadowed, and Emily was sound asleep on the queen-size bed, right between Lucas and Shelley. The three of them had come down after they settled things with ship security and snuggled on the bed, talking and making plans, until Emily had finally drifted off.

Then Shelley and Lucas talked in whispers, being close, holding hands, just enjoying being alive and relishing the miracle of finding each other.

"Are you sure about getting married?" Shelley asked softly, hating having to say the words but knowing that she had to get them out in case he'd offered in a moment of elation born out of surviving.

Lucas looked at her, his eyes shadowed, his fingertip tracing the line of her cheek. "Very sure," he whispered. "This is it for me. You and Emily. It's like finding a treasure that you didn't even know was waiting there for you until you uncovered it by accident."

"I thought you didn't like kids."

His finger trembled on her face. "I didn't. Until now. I didn't even like you before I met you."

She didn't look away. "And now?"

His hand brushed her hair. "Now?"

"That's the question, or do you want to stand on the fifth amendment?"

"Self-incrimination?" He drew back and looked at Emily. "I'm new at this, but will she be all right if we move?"

Shelley eased back and off the bed, then stood with her arms out at her sides. "See how easy it is?" she said.

Lucas followed her example, awkwardly managing to get off the bed without making too much movement, then he padded around to where she stood. He looked at her without touching her. "How about if we go into my cabin? Will she be afraid if she wakes up and you're gone?"

"Emily sleeps soundly. Nothing wakes her." She made contact by taking his hand and leading the way to the connecting door.

Once they stepped into the darkness of the other cabin, Shelley eased the door shut until it clicked softly. When she turned, Lucas was by the bed staring at the angel on the side table. She crossed to him and whispered, "Ashley looks as if she's bringing us all good luck."

He turned. "That's an understatement."

"How's your arm?" she asked.

"It hurts, but it's bearable."

"Then answer the question." She touched his chest, pressing her palms to the heat of his bare skin, and was surprised to find his heart racing under her touch. "I need to know. I need to hear you say it again."

He slipped his hand around her neck under her hair, warm and strong against her nape. "The truth is, I love you, Shelley Kingston."

Her hands stilled. He'd only said those words once before, and she knew that she'd never tire of hearing them. "Are you sure?" she asked.

"Oh, I'm very sure."

"I love you, too," she breathed as she pressed a kiss to his bare chest. She felt him tremble at the touch, and as she kissed his nipple, it hardened instantly. "And Emily's so excited about the wedding."

"Since the captain can do it at noon, everything's settled."

"I can't wait," she murmured as she tasted his skin. "A Christmas wedding with the sisters and the professor. It's too bad your brothers can't be here so one of them can be best man."

"Maybe Santa can be the best man," he said, his voice vaguely unsteady as her hands drifted lower on his body.

She undid the button on his pants, then slowly slid the zipper down. "Maybe he'll be too busy after all the work he's done tonight. Goodness knows he's worked overtime for all of us."

"I'll bribe him," Lucas said and drew in a sharp breath as she found evidence of how much he wanted her. "Can we do this?" he gasped.

"I can, how about you?" she murmured as she tugged the white cotton down.

"I don't think that's a problem," he said with a groan.

She felt him swelling even more under her touch. "That's definitely not a problem."

"But Emily—"

"Is sleeping. But I'm not, and you're here to protect me."

"From what?" he gasped as she made a trail of kisses down his chest to his abdomen.

"From losing my dreams," she whispered against his skin, then she moved to the bed and pulled him with her. As they fell onto the mussed linen that they'd left what seemed an eternity ago, Shelley snuggled close to Lucas. "I've just started to believe in dreams again, and I don't want to lose them."

"It's a big job to be the protector of dreams."

She raised herself on one elbow to look at him in the soft shadows. "You're the only one who can do it," she said. "But you've got to sign on forever."

"That's what I had in mind," he said, then buried his fingers in her hair and pulled her head to his. "This is going to be a very merry Christmas."

"Amen," Shelley breathed and as she caught a glimpse of the angel behind Lucas, she knew that she really did believe in miracles.

HARLEQUIN
AMERICAN ◆ ROMANCE ®

Once in a while, there's a man so special, a story so
different, that your pulse races, your blood rushes.
We call this

AMERICAN ROMANCE
heart beat

Jason Hill is one such man, and HEAVEN KNOWS is one such book.

To Sabrina, Jason was so special that not even death could take him away. She could still hear his laughter, see his beautiful face and feel his eyes on her. Was she mad...or was her husband still with her in their marriage bed?

HEAVEN KNOWS
by
TRACY HUGHES

Don't miss this exceptional, sexy hero. He'll make your HEARTBEAT!

Available in July wherever Harlequin books are sold.
Watch for more Heartbeat stories, coming your way soon!

MILLION DOLLAR SWEEPSTAKES (III)

No purchase necessary. To enter, follow the directions published. Method of entry may vary. For eligibility, entries must be received no later than March 31, 1996. No liability is assumed for printing errors, lost, late or misdirected entries. Odds of winning are determined by the number of eligible entries distributed and received. Prizewinners will be determined no later than June 30, 1996.

Sweepstakes open to residents of the U.S. (except Puerto Rico), Canada, Europe and Taiwan who are 18 years of age or older. All applicable laws and regulations apply. Sweepstakes offer void wherever prohibited by law. Values of all prizes are in U.S. currency. This sweepstakes is presented by Torstar Corp., its subsidiaries and affiliates, in conjunction with book, merchandise and/or product offerings. For a copy of the Official Rules send a self-addressed, stamped envelope (WA residents need not affix return postage) to: MILLION DOLLAR SWEEPSTAKES (III) Rules, P.O. Box 4573, Blair, NE 68009, USA.

EXTRA BONUS PRIZE DRAWING

No purchase necessary. The Extra Bonus Prize will be awarded in a random drawing to be conducted no later than 5/30/96 from among all entries received. To qualify, entries must be received by 3/31/96 and comply with published directions. Drawing open to residents of the U.S. (except Puerto Rico), Canada, Europe and Taiwan who are 18 years of age or older. All applicable laws and regulations apply; offer void wherever prohibited by law. Odds of winning are dependent upon number of eligibile entries received. Prize is valued in U.S. currency. The offer is presented by Torstar Corp., its subsidiaries and affiliates in conjunction with book, merchandise and/or product offering. For a copy of the Official Rules governing this sweepstakes, send a self-addressed, stamped envelope (WA residents need not affix return postage) to: Extra Bonus Prize Drawing Rules, P.O. Box 4590, Blair, NE 68009, USA.

SWP-H794

This summer, come cruising with Harlequin Books!

PORTS
OF CALL

In July, August and September, excitement, danger and, of course, romance can be found in Lynn Leslie's exciting new miniseries PORTS OF CALL. Not only can you cruise the South Pacific, the Caribbean and the Nile, your journey will also take you to Harlequin Superromance®, Harlequin Intrigue® and Harlequin American Romance®.

- ♦ In July, cruise the South Pacific with
  SINGAPORE FLING, a Harlequin Superromance
- ♦ NIGHT OF THE NILE from Harlequin Intrigue
  will heat up your August
- ♦ September is the perfect month for
  CRUISIN' MR. DIAMOND from
  Harlequin American Romance

So, cruise through the summer with LYNN LESLIE and HARLEQUIN BOOKS!

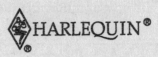

WEDDING SONG
Vicki Lewis Thompson

Kerry Muldoon has encountered more than her
share of happy brides and grooms. She and her
band—the Honeymooners—play at all the
wedding receptions held in romantic Eternity,
Massachusetts!

Kerry longs to walk down the aisle one day—
with sexy recording executive Judd Roarke. But
Kerry's dreams of singing stardom threaten to
tear apart the fragile fabric of their union....

WEDDING SONG, available in August
from Temptation, is the third book in
Harlequin's new cross-line series,
WEDDINGS, INC. Be sure to look for the
fourth book, **THE WEDDING GAMBLE,** by
Muriel Jensen (Harlequin American Romance
#549), coming in September.

HARLEQUIN®

AMERICAN ✦ ROMANCE®

"GOIN' TO THE CHAPEL"

American Romance is goin' to the chapel...with three soon-to-be-wed couples. Only thing is, saying "I do" is the farthest thing from their minds!

Be sure you haven't missed any of the nuptials. If you have, you can join us belatedly:

#16533	THE EIGHT SECOND WEDDING by Anne McAllister	$3.50	☐
#16537	THE KIDNAPPED BRIDE by Charlotte Maclay	$3.50	☐
#16541	VEGAS VOWS by Linda Randall Wisdom	$3.50	☐
	(limited quantities available)		

TOTAL AMOUNT	$
POSTAGE & HANDLING	$
($1.00 for one book, 50¢ for each additional)	
APPLICABLE TAXES*	$_____
TOTAL PAYABLE	$_____

(check or money order—please do not send cash)

To order, complete this form and send it, along with a check or money order for the total above, payable to Harlequin Books, to: **In the U.S.:** 3010 Walden Avenue, P.O. Box 9047, Buffalo, NY 14269-9047; **In Canada:** P.O. Box 613, Fort Erie, Ontario, L2A 5X3.

Name:_____

Address:_____City:_____

State/Prov.:_____Zip/Postal Code: _____

*New York residents remit applicable sales taxes.
 Canadian residents remit applicable GST and provincial taxes.

GTCF